For Peace of Mind

For Peace of Mind

A Pride and Prejudice Variation

LEENIE BROWN

Contents

Dedication

To my husband, the *love of my heart*

Chapter 1

Mr. Gardiner gave a small snort and shifted in his seat. Elizabeth glanced at her dozing uncle. She was glad to be in his carriage and moving away from Longbourn.

She tried to read the book that had lain open to the same page for the last half hour, but it was no use. Her mind would not stop repeating the events of the last few days. She sighed and looked out the window.

She had tried to avoid Mr. Collins, and aside from one dance at the Netherfield ball and those horrible few moments spent together a day ago, she had been successful. But it was those few moments confined in the breakfast room that had done the damage. Her cousin had managed to announce his intentions and had not been willing to accept her refusal. A great stir had arisen in the wake of her rejection, and now her mother steadfastly ignored her, save to complain loudly about her whenever she was near.

Her father had only tolerated the disturbance for a few hours before sending an express to request Mr. Gardiner's advanced arrival in Meryton and his willingness to return home with not just Jane but also Elizabeth. And so, Elizabeth Bennet sat in the carriage next to her sister. She had been sent away—sent away for her own good and her father's peace of mind.

Elizabeth closed her book and tucked it into her reticule. She studied her sister for a moment. Jane dabbed at her eyes, and Elizabeth gave her hand a small squeeze.

Jane smiled at her, but the smile did not reach her eyes. "I shall be well. A little time is all that is needed to get over a disappointment, or so I have been told."

"We have also been told to keep an eye out for husbands." Elizabeth spoke softly so as not to disturb her uncle. "I dare say if I do not return home with a prospect, Mama shall disown me and throw me into the hedgerows."

"She really was quite put out with you, was she

not?" Jane could not help the small chuckle that escaped her.

"Was?" Elizabeth huffed. "She still is."

Mr. Gardiner shifted again in his seat as the carriage began its halting journey through the streets of London. He yawned and stretched. "Your cousins will be glad to see you. Andrew has been planning a trip to the park with you, Lizzy. Margaret would like to have Jane help her with a bonnet. Michael has several stories already chosen for reading, and Amelia helped Cook make some special cakes for your arrival." He peered out the window. Elizabeth loved how anxious he was to be home. She wished that she could one day feel the same about her home.

Finally, the carriage rattled to a stop before the Gardiner's townhouse. A smile spread across Mr. Gardiner's face. "There, did I not tell you they would be eager to see you?"

Andrew was first to exit the house followed by Mrs. Gardiner and her three other children. The children shifted and danced behind their mother, eagerly waiting to greet their cousins.

"My dears, it is so good to see you." Mrs. Gardiner gave each girl a warm embrace as they alighted from the carriage. "As soon as the children have given you a proper welcome, we will have tea and cakes in the drawing room."

Three-year-old Michael bounced up and down. "Cake, cake, cake," he said grabbing Elizabeth's hand and pulling. "Mia make cake."

"So your father said," Elizabeth replied as she allowed herself to be pulled into the house.

The Gardeners did not live in a very fashionable section of town. Their house was modest but well-kept and comfortable. Uncle Gardiner ran a prosperous import and export business not far from his home and although he could afford to live in a more upscale district, preferred to stay close to his business and the friends that lived in the community. They employed several servants, and their children had a nurse and a governess. But, to the outside world, their address left them out of many circles.

Within these walls, a familial warmth radiated to everyone who entered as if the home had some magic to soothe even the weariest of individuals. But Elizabeth knew that it was not the building that held the magic, but the family within it. She watched as Amelia proudly and properly served her cakes, and Margaret poured tea under the supervision and instruction of her mother. She smiled with contentment.

After the children had had their treats and the attention of their favourite cousins for some time, they returned to the nursery, and Jane and Elizabeth were allowed to settle in and refresh before dinner. Elizabeth lay on the bed looking at the ceiling.

"It is nice to be here, is it not? I so love Aunt and Uncle and their children."

"As do I," said Jane as she joined her sister on the bed.

"If I ever get married and have a family, I would wish for a home like this. Full of love and welcoming."

Jane nodded her agreement. "I love Mama and Papa with all my heart, but theirs is not a marriage I wish to copy."

"Nor I," agreed Elizabeth. "I will only marry someone whom I love and respect and is my equal in intellect." Elizabeth sat up, "And, he cannot be the sort of man who does not encourage his wife to learn and read. I fear marriage for me is an impossibility!" She flopped back on the bed. "I am sure such a man does not exist! Instead, I will have to be satisfied to live with you and your family and care for your children. I will teach them to read and write and question everything they hear."

Jane grabbed a pillow and threw it at her. "I do not for one moment believe that you will be a spinster." She lay down on the bed next to Elizabeth. "But, I should love to have you live with me always."

Elizabeth rolled over and propped herself up on her elbows to look at Jane. "And because I love you, I will promise to teach your children some decorum so that they are not as silly as our younger sisters. I love Papa dearly, but I will never be diverted by my children's improprieties. I fear it is our family's unseemly behaviour that has brought you so much sorrow, dear sister." She scowled. "I am sure that arrogant man persuaded Mr. Bingley to leave because your connections were below him."

"Elizabeth," Jane chided. "You cannot go around making assumptions about the actions of others. You are far too hard on Mr. Darcy. If anyone is to blame, it is Mr. Bingley's horrid sister."

"Why Jane," said Elizabeth proudly, "I do

believe that is the most unkind thing you have ever said."

Jane smiled in response. "We should go to Aunt. I am sure she is waiting for us."

Downstairs, the Gardiners sat quietly talking in the drawing room as they waited for their nieces to join them for dinner. Jane and Elizabeth were favourites of the Gardiners and their children. Both girls were well-mannered and caring. Although Elizabeth could at times let her tongue and temper get the better of her, she was usually quick to right the wrong and worked diligently to keep herself under good regulation. Jane was sweet to a fault. Steady and easy-going, she was quick to find the good in all and in all situations. The two girls balanced each other perfectly. Elizabeth challenged Jane to take risks while Jane calmed Elizabeth and helped to soothe her when she became irritated.

"Do you know any gentlemen to whom we might introduce our nieces while they are in town?"

Mr. Gardiner scrunched up his face and rubbed his chin while he thought. "There is my former partner's son. He is to come to dinner tomorrow. I should think he would do quite well with Jane, and perhaps he has a strong-minded friend he might be willing to introduce to our Lizzy." He laughed softly. "It would have to be a very strong-minded young man. Matlock's nephew comes to mind, but I am not sure Matlock would wish a connection to trade."

"My dear, I may be partial, but any gentleman with good sense and an eye for prosperity should beg for a connection to you."

Mr. Gardiner patted his wife's hand. "I quite like your partiality, my love." He stood and offered his arm to her as his nieces entered the drawing room followed by his three eldest children. "I believe dinner awaits."

~*~*~*~*~

"What say you, girls? I have planned to visit some shops tomorrow. Shall we make a day of it and stop for some chocolate and scones? We can be ladies of leisure for a day," suggested Mrs. Gardiner as dinner drew to a close.

"Oh, I so enjoy visiting the shops," cooed Jane.

Elizabeth grimaced playfully. "I think I can bear it if I am in your company, Aunt."

Jane gave her sister's arm a playful swat. "Oh, Elizabeth, you like shopping and chocolate."

"But," whined Andrew the Gardiner's five-year-old son, "I want to go to the park."

"Andrew," Mr. Gardiner spoke sternly. "You are not to whine. A boy who always demands his own way does not grow up to be a fine gentleman."

Andrew lowered his eyes and pushed his final carrot around his plate before chewing it carefully while he thought. Then, he straightened in his chair and addressed Elizabeth in his most proper voice. "Cousin Elizabeth, would you please take me to the park on a day that is not tomorrow?" He spun to look at his father. "Is that better, Papa? Can I still grow up to be a fine gentleman and go to the park?"

Mr. Gardiner chuckled. "Much improved, son. And, I believe you can go to the park and still be a gentleman. "

Elizabeth smiled at the young boy whose eyes implored her to grant his wish. "I would be delighted to accompany a fine young gentleman to the park the day after tomorrow," said Elizabeth.

Jumping up, Andrew rushed over to Elizabeth's chair but stopped abruptly at her side. "Papa, it is not proper for gentlemen to hug ladies, is it? Elizabeth is a lady, but may I still hug her?"

"Well, Andrew, since Elizabeth is your cousin, and you are still only a very young gentleman, it is permissible."

Andrew threw his arms around his cousin and said, "Thank you, Lizzy."

Elizabeth returned the hug. "Would you like to choose a story for me to read tonight?"

Andrew nodded his head vigorously.

She looked at her uncle who gave a small nod allowing her to dismiss the children from the table.

"Then off with you," she said. "I shall be up in an hour to tuck you in and read your story."

Andrew raced off followed by his siblings.

~*~*~*~*~*~

The ladies had spent a leisurely morning attending one store and then another. They bought ribbons, lace, buttons and fabric, as well as a pair of gloves and some new stockings before stopping at a tea shop for some refreshments.

"Delightful." Jane sighed with pleasure as she sipped her chocolate and nibbled her scone.

Elizabeth suddenly began to sputter. Grabbing

her chocolate, she drank some hoping to calm her coughing.

"You should be more careful," chided Jane. "We cannot have you expiring from choking on a scone and chocolate."

Elizabeth gave a wry smile. "I was merely startled. Apparently, you should not gasp when you are eating."

"Startled, by what?" asked Jane.

"Not by what — by whom."

Jane gave her a puzzled look. "What do you mean?"

"I mean Mr. Darcy is here." Elizabeth grabbed her sister's arm to stop her from looking toward the door. "Do not turn around. We do not want him to see us, or we shall be forced to speak to him."

"Lizzy, you are being ridiculous! I believe you spoke to him quite well while you were at Netherfield. You told me of your many discussions."

"We did not discuss, Jane; we argued."

"It was still speaking," insisted Jane. She cautiously turned—ever so slightly—to see the gentleman looking for someone. Darcy nodded toward a gentleman sitting just behind Elizabeth. "Lizzy, he is coming this way. I think he is meeting with the officer at the table behind us. Prepare yourself to speak to him."

At that moment, Darcy was striding purposefully toward his cousin but stopped short of his destination when he saw Elizabeth.

"Miss Bennet, Miss Elizabeth," he said with a bow. "It is good to see you again."

"Thank you, Mr. Darcy," said Elizabeth.

"It is good to see you again, too, sir," added Jane. "This is our aunt, Mrs. Edward Gardiner. We are visiting with the Gardiners while in town."

"Edward Gardiner?" Darcy drew his eyebrows together in a quizzical expression.

"Yes, Mr. Darcy. Edward Gardiner is my uncle. Do you know him?" asked Elizabeth.

"Yes, he and I work together on a regular basis. I had no idea he was your uncle."

"He is my mother's brother. I believe you heard that we had relatives in Cheapside." Elizabeth gave him an arch smile.

Darcy narrowed his eyes slightly and lifted an eyebrow while trying to repress a smile. "Yes, I did, but I never put that information together with Mr. Gardiner. There are many people who reside near Cheapside."

Mrs. Gardiner watched the exchange with interest while Jane smiled behind her cup.

"I, too have come here to meet a relation today. Richard, come meet some friends of mine. " There was a scuffling of a chair and the officer at the other table approached Darcy. "Richard, this is Miss Bennet and Miss Elizabeth Bennet of Longbourn in Hertfordshire, and this is their aunt, Mrs. Edward Gardiner. Ladies, this is my cousin, Colonel Richard Fitzwilliam."

"Mr. Edward Gardiner?"

"The very same, cousin."

"It is a pleasure to meet you, ladies. I believe I know your husband quite well, Mrs. Gardiner," said Richard.

"Fitzwilliam, is it?" asked Mrs. Gardiner. "Second son of Lord Matlock?"

"The one and only." Richard gave an exaggerated bow.

Mrs. Gardiner smiled. "I have heard several interesting tales about you and your cousin — which I assume must be you, Mr. Darcy?"

Darcy grimaced and nodded. "I am afraid so."

"No need to be alarmed gentlemen. None of those stories shall pass my lips without severe provocation. Though they are quite diverting." She motioned to an empty seat at the table. "Please join us. We will not be much longer, and then we will leave you to your business."

Elizabeth's eyes twinkled as she turned to Richard. "Colonel, you must provoke her. I would so love to hear a story that makes Mr. Darcy's face take on that peculiar shade of grey."

Richard laughed and pulled up a chair. "Sit, Darcy. It is not often that we have such lovely company when we stop here."

"You come here often?" Jane asked.

"I would say regularly. About twice a week, is that not so, Darcy?" Darcy nodded his agreement. "Sometimes it is just the two of us, and sometimes it is one of my fellow soldiers or Darcy's friend Bingley, but none of them are as lovely as you ladies," charmed Richard.

"You flatter us," said Elizabeth with a smile as she took a sip of her chocolate. After a moment of silence, she added with a pointed look at Mr. Darcy, "Please do not stop, Colonel. Every lady loves to be flattered."

Richard chuckled while Darcy looked flustered. "What brings you ladies out on this fine day?"

"What we women do best — shopping," said Mrs. Gardiner. "Today, we are pretending to be ladies of leisure for a few hours before we have to return to being ladies of responsibility."

Darcy smiled at the comment. "And has it been a successful enterprise, Mrs. Gardiner?"

"Oh, very, Mr. Darcy. There shall be much stitching to be done in the following days — dresses to be altered, bonnets to be trimmed, things that bore my good husband to tears but occupy many of my hours. However, we are not finished. We have two more shops to visit before we return home."

"And are those a secret not meant for gentlemanly ears?" whispered the Colonel leaning forward.

"Oh, yes, sir," Elizabeth whispered back, leaning towards him. "We would not want anyone to know that there are ladies who would visit a bookseller or a sweets shop, now would we?"

"Most definitely not," agreed the Colonel with mock gravity.

"Lizzy has been waiting all day to visit those shops," said Jane. "We knew if we let her go to the booksellers first, we would never get to the other stores. And the sweets are for our cousins. Lizzy and I like to spoil them a bit when we come to visit. So, today they will get sweets and a story and tomorrow, the girls will get to use some of the things we bought to alter dresses and bonnets. Then we will all go to the park, and Aunt Gardiner will get to relax."

"We like to spoil her, too." Lizzy grinned at her aunt.

"I like to think of it as paying me back for all the troubles you caused as a youngster, Lizzy," her aunt teased.

"So, Miss Elizabeth was the only one to cause troubles, was she, Miss Bennet?" quizzed Richard.

"Usually," said Jane. "Still does to some degree. That is why Andrew loves her so. She is his favourite cousin. He even says he is going to marry her someday."

"But," Elizabeth added, "he is only five, and I will be old and haggard by the time he is old enough."

"I doubt you will ever be old and haggard, Elizabeth," said Mrs. Gardiner. "And he will love you just as well then as he does now." She patted her niece's hand affectionately. "They really do have a special bond."

Elizabeth coloured slightly. "He is my favourite, but you mustn't tell Michael, Amelia or Margaret."

Colonel Fitzwilliam pretended to lock his lips and throw away the key. "We military men are good at keeping secrets."

"Most of the time," muttered Darcy.

"Darcy, I was eight. I was not in the military yet, so I cannot be held accountable for telling on you."

"Well, if that were the only time, I suppose it could be overlooked, but then there was the time when we were twelve, and when we were sixteen—you shall remain in my debt for some time for that one—and then when we were in Italy and just last week you told Georgiana..."

Richard held up his hands in defense. "You have made your point, Darcy. I am a terrible secret keeper when it comes to you. Must your memory be so good?"

"Yes, I think it must." A slight smile pulled at the corners of his mouth.

Elizabeth watched the interaction between the gentlemen with interest. It clashed with the image she held of the dour Mr. Darcy. This Mr. Darcy was likeable, and that smile was adorable. Elizabeth took a final sip of her chocolate and studied his face.

"Miss Elizabeth? Do you have a question?" Darcy was a little unnerved by the intense scrutiny.

"No, Mr. Darcy. I am still merely trying to take a sketch of your character. Every time I think I have it taken, you change. Colonel Fitzwilliam, is he always this frustrating?"

"Usually," said Richard.

"Well, gentlemen," Mrs. Gardiner placed her empty cup on the table, "we must take our leave of you if we are to finish our shopping before dinner. It has been a pleasure to meet you both and finally put a face to the name, so to speak." She stood. "Mr. Gardiner and I would welcome you to call on us anytime. Jane and Elizabeth will be with us until Christmastime."

"Or until Mama forgives me," muttered Elizabeth.

"Elizabeth!" hissed Jane.

Darcy ignored the exchange though he could not help but wonder why Elizabeth's mother was angry with her.

"Could we impose upon you tomorrow when

you go to the park with the children, ladies? I would very much like to meet the gentleman who has stolen Miss Elizabeth's heart," said Richard. Both he and Jane looked to Mrs. Gardiner for her consent.

Mrs. Gardiner nodded her approval of the scheme and Jane said as she fastened her wrap, "That would be lovely. Shall we say one o'clock?"

"And perhaps you could return with the girls to take tea with me?" asked Mrs. Gardiner. "I shall be quite desirous of the company after an afternoon of solitude."

The gentlemen agreed and bowed as the ladies took their leave.

Chapter 2

As soon as the ladies had exited the building, Richard rounded on his cousin, "Would you care to enlighten me on your relationship with Miss Elizabeth?"

"I have no relationship with the Bennets beyond a passing acquaintance," said Darcy defensively. "I met Miss Elizabeth and her sister when I was in Hertfordshire with Bingley."

"Bingley..." Richard tapped his lip with his finger while he studied his cousin. There was a slight red tinge to Darcy's ears–a sign he had often relied on to know when his cousin was holding back information and giving him only the barest of truths. There was one way to piece together the information he sought. He snapped his fingers as if he had just had a brilliant idea, and though he doubted it to be true, he announced, "She is Bingley's angel."

"Miss Elizabeth?" Darcy's eyes grew wide in astonishment. "No, Bingley's angel is Miss Bennet."

"Ah, that makes more sense," said Richard, pleased that his tactics seemed to be working. "So, Miss Elizabeth is the lady Miss Bingley spoke of who appeared at Netherfield in a state of wildness having walked an unladylike distance. "

"Yes, Miss Bingley does like to speak ill of Miss Elizabeth."

"So, you like Miss Elizabeth." Richard leaned back in his chair, folding his arms across his chest in a satisfied fashion.

"How do you figure?"

"Miss Bingley disapproves of Miss Elizabeth, and you could not keep your eyes off of her while we spoke. There is only one logical conclusion. Miss Bingley is jealous, and you are smitten."

Unwilling to carry that particular conversation any further, Darcy shrugged and ordered another coffee as Bingley walked in.

"Bingley, my good man," said Richard. "I just met your angel and her sister."

Darcy rolled his eyes and shook his head. He knew what his cousin was about.

"Miss Bennet is here in London?" Bingley looked about the room as if he expected to see her.

"Yes, and Miss Elizabeth, too," said Darcy.

"Seems their uncle is Mr. Edward Gardiner, and they are staying with him until Christmas-time," said Richard.

"Or until Miss Elizabeth's mother forgives her for something," added Darcy.

"You heard that too? That is one of the reasons I wanted to meet with them tomorrow. I need to know what she has done."

"You are far too curious for your own good, Richard," said Darcy flatly.

Bingley's cup halted in the air and slowly returned to the table. "Mr. Edward Gardiner is Miss Bennet's uncle?" Bingley was incredulous. "My father's former business partner—the one who bought him out?"

"The same," said Darcy. "Lives near Cheapside, it seems."

"Yes, I know. I have been to his house on many occasions. In fact, I am to join the Gardiners for dinner tonight." Bingley smirked at Darcy. "Are Miss Bennet's connections still too low?"

Richard's eyes grew wide. "You told him Miss Bennet's connections were too low?"

Darcy nodded.

"A gentleman's daughter..."

"With ties to trade," added Darcy.

"Ah, yes, trade. One would not wish to keep company with someone connected to trade." Richard scoffed.

Darcy cast a sidelong glance at Bingley. "I am not speaking of merely keeping company with someone connected with trade, Richard."

"Marriage?" Richard looked first to Bingley, who gave him a nod and then leaned in to study his cousin's face. "Worried that Bingley would be connected to trade or that you would be?"

Bingley snorted.

Darcy narrowed his eyes and glared at his all-too-perceptive cousin. "You have not met the rest of her family."

"Derbyshire is near Hertfordshire?"

"You know it is not."

"But, apparently, you have forgotten."

Bingley sighed loudly, putting an end to the

discussion that threatened to become heated. "What do I do?"

"About what?" asked Richard.

"About dinner tonight at the Gardiner's?"

"You eat," said Richard. Then, seeing the glares of both men, he held up his hands in defense and returned to his coffee.

"Does your sister know you dine in Cheapside?" asked Darcy.

"No, she only knows I dine with Father's former partner."

"It might be best if you keep it that way," cautioned Darcy and the three gentlemen laughed.

"If she only knew that a relative of the Bennets is responsible for our rise from trade," said Bingley. "I do not know what she would do. If she becomes too annoying, I may have to tell her."

"Please, let us be there if you do," pleaded Richard.

"Richard," hissed Darcy.

"You know you would like to see it too, Darcy," said Bingley. "It would be quite the spectacle. However, for now, she will not know of it or the Bennets being in town. I do not think I can take any more of her diatribes about Miss Elizabeth and her family."

"He likes her, you know." Richard inclined his head towards Darcy.

"Yes, I know. The only people unaware of that fact are Darcy and Miss Elizabeth," laughed Bingley.

Darcy glowered at his friend. He drummed his fingers on the table as he often did when contemplating something of great importance. Finally, he spoke in a resigned tone. "She heard me, Bingley."

"Oh, Darcy! When will you learn to hold your tongue?"

"When you stop pestering me to do something when I do not wish to do it."

"What did she hear?" asked Richard.

"How do you know?" asked Bingley.

"Something she said today when talking to Richard about flattery. She looked me in the eye and said ladies like to be flattered," replied Darcy, ignoring his cousin's question.

"What did she hear?" Richard's patience was waning.

"She definitely heard you." Bingley also ignored Richard's question. "I suppose both of us should apologize for that."

"What. did. she. hear?" Richard spoke through clenched teeth.

"You know if we do not tell him, he will just ask her," commented Bingley.

"I know, but can we not ignore him for a bit longer?" asked Darcy.

"I am right here. I can hear you. Now one of you tell me what she said, or I will find the bookseller's shop." Richard moved to get up.

"Sit down, Richard, I shall tell you. Darcy here was unhappy to be at an assembly with me in Meryton. A royal grump, he was that night. I suggested he dance."

"He insisted I should dance and then suggested partners for me," grumbled Darcy.

"I suggested Miss Bennet's sister, Miss Elizabeth. Without looking to see who she was or what she looked like and without noticing she was standing quite near, he announced she was tolerable, but not handsome enough to tempt him. Of course, he spent the rest of the night staring at her." Bingley rolled his eyes, and Richard laughed.

"That sounds like my cousin when he is in a mood. I suppose he scowled all night, too?"

"Indeed, he did."

"I am sitting right here; I can hear you."

"We know," said Richard with a wink. "So how should we go about arranging the match, Bingley?"

"I do not think Bingley is in a favourable position presently either, Richard."

"No, I left the neighbourhood rather abruptly due to legitimate business in town, but then your cousin, my sisters, and Mr. Hurst left, too. And according to Hurst — he hears much while he sleeps." Both Darcy and Richard chuckled for they had witnessed Hurst's escape from female conversation by feigning sleep on many occasions. "Caroline sent a letter to Miss Bennet telling her I was not coming back and insinuating I was reserved for Georgiana." Bingley looked at Richard levelly.

"Georgiana?" asked Richard.

"Yes, that is what Caroline said," replied Bingley. "Absurd is it not. Lovely as she is, Georgiana is like a younger sister to me, not a marriage candidate."

"Are you certain you do not wish to tell your sister about the Bennets' connection to your family?" queried Richard.

"It is tempting," said Bingley. "But I think I will hold on to that information a bit longer. Now, back to my question, what do I do about tonight's dinner?"

"Go, be Bingley," said Darcy, "Perhaps you will get a chance to explain yourself, but I am going to caution you. Jane and Elizabeth are favourite nieces of the Gardiners."

"Of course they are. Why would life be easy?" Bingley threw his hands up in exasperation.

"If anyone can come through something like this, Bingley, it is you," encouraged Richard. "Your task is not as difficult as Darcy's. You only need to apologize for a meddling sister while Darcy has to apologize for being—Darcy in a bad mood."

~*~*~*~*~*~

"I do not understand why you have spoken so ill of Mr. Darcy, Elizabeth. He is a fine gentleman. I did not see anything overly proud about his demeanor today, and he is a favourite with your uncle. Mr. Gardiner only bestows his favour on the truly worthy, you know."

Elizabeth furrowed her brows in confusion. "The Mr. Darcy today was completely different from the Mr. Darcy I met in Hertfordshire." Indeed, today's Mr. Darcy was most agreeable.

"I did not find him different," said Jane. "But,

I am not the one whose pride got wounded by a hasty comment."

"What comment was that?" asked Mrs. Gardiner.

"She is tolerable, but not handsome enough to tempt me," quoted Elizabeth.

"It was at an assembly, Aunt. Mr. Bingley was attempting to persuade Mr. Darcy to dance. Mr. Darcy was in a foul mood and spoke in haste, I am sure of it since he could not keep his eyes off Lizzy for the rest of the night. I would say he finds her more than tolerable."

"So, you are holding a grudge over a remark made without a moment's forethought? That hardly seems very fair."Mrs. Gardiner chided Elizabeth as they entered the book shop.

Elizabeth carefully studied the floor in front of her feet. It did seem foolish to hold onto one slight for so long.

"I can remember some of your uncle's stories about Colonel Fitzwilliam and Mr. Darcy, and I can assure you it is not the first time Mr. Darcy has been annoyed into saying something he regretted." Mrs. Gardiner slipped her arm through Elizabeth's and pulled her close to her side. "From what I hear, the Colonel enjoys tormenting his cousin at times. While I found Colonel Fitzwilliam most entertaining, I could see how his jovial nature might annoy a reserved person like Mr. Darcy. Can you see that?"

Elizabeth nodded. "I can see that."

"Then, I suggest you give Mr. Darcy a fresh start," counselled her aunt.

Elizabeth sighed and nodded slowly. She knew her aunt was right. She had allowed her injured pride to prejudice her against Mr. Darcy. "I will forget what he said that night."

"And what of Mr. Wickham's stories? Will you also forget them?" asked Jane.

Mrs. Gardiner who had pulled a book from the shelf nearly dropped it upon hearing Jane's comment. "George Wickham?"

"Yes," said both of her nieces.

"Do not under any circumstance believe that man," said Mrs. Gardiner severely. "I cannot tell you why, but you must believe me. He is not to be trusted." The uncharacteristic firmness in her voice startled her nieces.

Jane looked at Elizabeth and then at her aunt's grave expression. "You might ask Uncle to write Papa then, Aunt. Mr. Wickham is stationed in

Meryton at present, and you know Kitty and Lydia when it comes to officers."

"I will have him write to your father directly," said Mrs. Gardiner. "Many have suffered at the hands of that man." She lowered her voice. "Mr. Darcy is one of them, and his suffering has been of a long duration—since they were children growing up in Derbyshire."

Elizabeth gasped. "You know, Aunt, he was showing particular attention to me, so I am glad you have told me."

Mrs. Gardiner clutched Jane's arm as if she needed it for support. "Jane, from your observations in Hertfordshire, would you have said Mr. Darcy admires Elizabeth?"

Jane nodded, her aunt's intensity was unsettling. "I believe he is half in love with her if not completely so."

"Is there any chance Mr. Wickham would have noticed Mr. Darcy's admiration for Elizabeth?" Panic filled her voice.

"No, I do not believe there is. They were not in company much."

"Good." Mrs. Gardiner sighed in relief and then, refocusing on the task at hand, she held up two books. "Now, which of these books do you wish to read to the children?"

Parcel in hand, they left the bookshop and headed to the sweets shop.

"Do you think we should pick out some treats for when we are at the park tomorrow?" asked Elizabeth. "It might be a good thing to have for the way home."

"I have found bribery works well with my children. I would take some along if I were you. And throw in a few extra for the big boys that are planning to meet you as well," said Mrs. Gardiner with a laugh. "Now, we are having company for dinner this evening, so we should get home to prepare."

"Who is coming?" asked Elizabeth.

"The son of your uncle's former business partner, Mr. Bingley," said Mrs. Gardiner.

"Mr. Bingley? A Mr. Charles Bingley is coming to dinner?" Elizabeth nearly shouted while Jane stood stock still.

"Yes, do you know him?" asked their aunt.

"Aunt, he has let Netherfield," said Elizabeth.

Shock suffused Mrs. Gardiner's face. "Oh, your uncle said he was just back from his home in the country to meet with him on business, but I did not realize his country home was Netherfield!"

"You said he truly came to town for business?" asked Jane.

"Yes, he had an important meeting with your uncle last week. I think the details were being finalized this morning. My understanding was that he was coming to dinner tonight and leaving for the country again on the morrow."

"He was returning to Netherfield?" asked Elizabeth incredulously.

"That is my understanding."

"But, Miss Bingley said he was not returning, You saw her letter, Lizzy. I did not misread it, did I?"

"You cannot misread he will not be returning until spring if at all. That is pretty clear to me. So, it is Miss Bingley, not Mr. Bingley, who jilted you!"

"So this Mr. Bingley is special?"

"I believe he may become my brother at some point, Aunt," Elizabeth replied with a grin. "His father was Uncle's business partner?"

"Yes, Edward bought Mr. Bingley out a few years ago before he passed away. Mr. Bingley's father used the money to move his children out of the trade business and into the realm of landed gentlemen. I understand he also used it to top off his daughters' dowries."

"But, Aunt, Uncle is not rich, and the Bingleys are," said Elizabeth.

"Who said he is not rich? Your uncle is very successful. His income, if he chose to take it, would rival the Bingleys'."

Elizabeth gasped. "In truth?"

"In truth," assured her Aunt. "Although his income is sufficient for a very comfortable life, it could be much higher. Your uncle does not choose to live on all the profits from his business. He instead has tucked much of it away to assist people and to grow his business. Your mother does not know it, but if Mr. Collins does ask her to leave Longbourn after your father's passing, your uncle, along with your father, have arranged to give her a manageable living and home. He and I did not want you or Jane or any of the other girls to have to marry out of necessity. We planned to tell you when you were old enough. In fact, after what happened with Mr. Collins, your uncle was going to speak to you about it while you were here."

"So, my refusing Mr. Collins is not the tragedy

Mama thinks it to be." Elizabeth chuckled and then dissolved into a fit of laughter.

"What is so funny, Lizzy?" asked Jane.

"Can you imagine the shock on Miss Bingley's face if she knew that part of her dowry and the leasing of Netherfield could be credited to our family?"

"Miss Bingley does not like you, Jane?"

"No, she thinks she is above us. But it is Lizzy she truly despises."

"Why does she hate Lizzy?"

"Because Miss Bingley has set her cap for Mr. Darcy, and Mr. Darcy likes Lizzy. Therefore, Lizzy and all of her relations are targets of Miss Bingley's ridicule."

"Ah, and we come back to Mr. Darcy and Lizzy. Something must be done about those two, do you not think?"

"Yes, Aunt. Something must be done." Mrs. Gardiner and Jane laughed at the scowl on Elizabeth's face.

~*~*~*~*~*~

"So, my Mr. Bingley is already Jane's admirer?" asked Mr. Gardiner of his wife when they met in their private sitting area before going down for dinner.

"Apparently so," replied his wife. "And your Mr. Darcy seems to admire our other favourite niece. We met Mr. Darcy and Colonel Fitzwilliam today at the tea shop. The man could not take his eyes off of Lizzy to be sure, but Lizzy is set against him at present. Has to do with a slighting remark he made when being pushed by Mr. Bingley to do something he did not want to do."

"That sounds like Darcy. So, you say he admires Lizzy?" Mr. Gardiner chuckled. "Seems that gentleman likes to be surrounded by trying people."

"Now, dear, it is Lizzy of whom we speak," admonished his wife.

"You and I both know that she can be trying. Knowing Mr. Darcy as I do—always in charge, ordered and serious—and knowing Lizzy as I do—never wishing to be told what to do and given to impulse—it would be a fun relationship to watch. And a very good one, too, I should think. Both girls would pair equally as well with those two gentlemen."

"I have not yet seen Mr. Bingley in company with Jane, but from what I saw of Mr. Darcy, he would be perfect for our Lizzy. I think she finds him interesting. She was entertained by the Colonel, and they fell into conversation quite readily, but there is something about Mr. Darcy she finds compelling. You could see it in her eyes and hear it in her challenging tone. She may have looked like she was flirting with the Colonel, but I believe she was really flirting with Mr. Darcy. She just does not realize it yet," said Mrs. Gardiner. "You know how she has strong reactions to most people, but this..."

"More intense? Is that possible?" asked Mr. Gardiner in surprise. "This I would love to see, indeed—perhaps another dinner with more guests than Mr. Bingley next week?"

"Perfectly fine with me, my love. But tonight's dinner may be just as interesting. It seems Mr. Bingley's sister told Jane that Mr. Bingley was not returning to Netherfield. Since Mr. Bingley had departed suddenly for a business meeting, Jane thought that he had jilted her. It could be a bit awkward tonight, my dear, and if it is not, I am afraid you may have lost your conversation partner."

"I do not think I could be sad to lose out on conversation for such a lovely reason as Jane's happiness, Madeline." Mr. Gardiner pulled his wife into his embrace for a quick kiss. "Shall we go down and prepare for the entertainment?"

Jane and Elizabeth were sitting in the parlour amusing the children when the Gardiners entered the room.

"Mama," cried three-year-old Michael hopping out of Jane's lap and racing to his mother. She scooped him up and gave him a kiss on his plump cheek. Then, wiggling and giggling, he squirmed his way free and ran back to sit with Jane.

"Good evening, children," said Mr. Gardiner. He took a moment to address each one with a hug and kiss and a question about their day. They told him about their lessons and the games that they played.

"Lizzy and Jane have a treat for us after dinner, Papa," said Amelia. "They stopped at the sweets shop, and after supper, if we are good, we might have it." Her almost eight-year-old eyes were full of excited anticipation.

"And tomorrow, Jane has some ribbons she thinks will match my dress," said twelve-year-old Margaret.

"And, I get to go to the park," said Andrew. "And Lizzy has some friends that are going to come to meet me, Papa. She says they are friends of yours just like Mr. Bingley is."

"Friends?" asked Mr. Gardiner with a raised eyebrow and a mischievous look at his niece. "Gentleman friends?"

"Yes, Uncle, friends—nothing more," Elizabeth gave her uncle a peck on the cheek.

"At least nothing more for now," whispered Jane as she too greeted her uncle with a kiss.

Mr. Gardiner threw his head back in laughter and gave Jane an approving pat on the back. When he finally stopped laughing, he said to Jane, "I believe we have a gentleman friend of yours coming over this evening. Your aunt has been filling me in on your excursions and conversations from today. But, I must say, Madeline, you did not mention gentlemen friends joining my nieces and children at the park. Who might these gentlemen be? The ones you met at the tea shop?" He winked at Lizzy.

"Yes, Edward, Mr. Darcy and Colonel Fitzwilliam."

"Mr. Bingley," announced Roberts, the Gardiner's butler.

"Good evening, Mr. Bingley," said Mr. Gardiner. "Our party is larger than normal tonight. We have our nieces visiting with us from Hertfordshire, but they tell me they already know you, so I will forego the introductions."

"Indeed, we have met. Miss Bennet, Miss Elizabeth, it is a pleasure to see you again. I had not thought I would see you until the day after tomorrow as I was to return to Netherfield in the morning."

"It is good to see you again, too, Mr. Bingley," said Elizabeth. "We had not thought we would see you again until at least spring."

Bingley smiled. "Ah, my sister must have told you that." Elizabeth nodded. "Country life does not suit her as well as it suits me." He laughed softly. "I could never abandon any of my friends either here or in the country. So, my plans have had to change. Darcy cannot get away at present, and since he was to accompany me, I will be waiting to return to Netherfield until he is available. I had been disappointed in the disruptions of my plans, but perhaps I can call on you ladies while I wait for him to finish up his business? It would make waiting so much more tolerable."

"Of course, you must call on us," said Elizabeth. "It is always pleasant to spend time with friends."

"Indeed it is," agreed Jane, a slight blush colouring her cheeks.

Mr. Gardiner winked at his wife, and she responded with a knowing smile.

"But tomorrow we are going to the park," said Andrew grabbing Elizabeth's hand and standing just a bit between her and Mr. Bingley.

"Yes, Andrew, tomorrow, we will go to the park. I gave you my promise, did I not?" Elizabeth smiled down at the youngster.

"Yes, Lizzy, and a lady or gentleman never goes back on a promise." He nodded his head gravely.

"Exactly. Now, would you, kind sir, do me the honour of walking me into dinner before returning to the nursery?" Elizabeth asked with a curtsey.

A smile suffused Andrew's face as he made an awkward bow and extended his arm to Elizabeth.

Mr. and Mrs. Gardiner led the way, followed by Andrew and Elizabeth while Mr. Bingley offered his arm to Jane.

"Andrew is learning to be a gentleman, and is quite in love with Lizzy," explained Jane. "I am afraid he was a bit jealous of your conversation with her."

"There is no need for him to fear on that regard, Miss Bennet, but, tell me, has he such feeling for you?" said Mr. Bingley in a low voice. "For if he does, then I may indeed be jealous."

Chapter 3

"Lizzy, are you ready to go to the park?" Andrew shifted from one foot to the other in eager anticipation of the outing.

Elizabeth ruffled his hair. Truth be told, he was not the only one anxious for the outing — and not merely for the sake of the exercise it afforded. "I need my pelisse, and you need your hat and gloves. The air is crisp today."

"Glubs, glubs, glubs." Michael waggled his gloves in front of her. She took them and helped him get his fingers in the right places.

Elizabeth smiled with satisfaction as she fastened her pelisse. "I think we are all ready to go. Four children, one governess, one maid, and two visiting cousins. Oh, and a treat for later." She held up a small parcel causing the children to clap their hands in glee.

"Good luck," said Mrs. Gardiner. "Give my greetings to the gentlemen, and remind them that I expect them to call. A warm cup of tea will be welcome after an outing in the park."

As the group of adults and children from Gracechurch Street wove their way through the streets of London in Mr. Gardiner's carriage, a trio of gentlemen was climbing into Darcy's carriage in another part of town.

"So, Bingley, the dinner went well?" asked Darcy.

"Very well, my friend, very well. I was invited to join you on your outing to the park, was I not?" asked a beaming Bingley. "I understand you wish to meet Master Andrew, Colonel?"

"'Twas the excuse," said Richard. "Though I do hope to find out why Miss Elizabeth said she was here until her mother forgave her. And, it seemed like a good way to throw the unsuspecting couple together." He winked at Darcy.

"Well, Darcy, you may wish to tread carefully. Master Andrew has laid claim to Miss Elizabeth. Stood between us when I was speaking to her last evening and never left her side until it was time to go back to the nursery," said Bingley.

"Thank you for the warning. I shall try not to get called out," said Darcy dryly.

"Uh, Darcy?" Bingley started cautiously.

"Yes."

"There is something else of which you should be warned. Hmmm. Let me see, how do I put this? Errr. Seeing Miss Elizabeth with the children could be somewhat distracting."

"Distracting? What are you talking about, Bingley?"

"Well, seeing Jane with little Michael on her lap last night made my mind wander to the possibilities in the future."

"Oh," said Darcy.

"Miss Bennet was interacting with the children so sweetly–it was quite a beguiling picture. But Miss Elizabeth, well, she really gets into playing with them, and they follow her around like little ducklings. And they seem to have her colouring as well. I thought you should be prepared."

Richard chortled. "Oh, this is an even better idea than I thought."

"Thank you, Bingley. It is good to see I have some friends who care about my well-being." Darcy glared at his cousin.

"Oh, I have your well-being in mind, too. Pemberley needs a mistress; you need a wife; and I have never, in all my years of going to balls and parties and plays and various other soirees, met a woman more suited to you than Miss Elizabeth," said Richard in a serious tone.

The carriage had arrived at the park just as the Gardiner party was coming down the street. Elizabeth had Michael on her hip; his curly dark head snuggled into her shoulder. Andrew's hand was clasped firmly in hers as he occasionally looked up to her, his head tilting slightly, obviously asking a question. Jane and the girls followed behind, Amelia occasionally tugging at Elizabeth's sleeve to get her attention. Darcy sat frozen, his jaw slack. He had never seen a more beautiful sight. His heart was racing. Richard was right. He did need a wife, a particular wife.

"I told you," said Bingley with a twinkle in his eye.

Darcy just nodded mutely, and Richard gave him a sound slap on the back and a playful grin. "I shall get out first, Cousin, so you can pull yourself together." And with that, Richard climbed out of the carriage followed by an eager Bingley and a somewhat shaky Darcy.

"Good afternoon, gentlemen," Elizabeth greeted them as they approached. "Allow me to introduce you to our group. First, this is Master Michael in my arms and Master Gardiner has a firm grasp on my hand." Michael hid his eyes shyly behind the collar of Elizabeth's pelisse, and Andrew practiced a bow. "Come forward, girls," instructed Elizabeth. Immediately, the girls came forward, one standing on either side of Elizabeth. "Next to Andrew is Miss Gardiner. And on my left is Miss Amelia." Both girls curtseyed. "We also have Miss Eddington, their governess, and Miss Lucy, their maid. Children, these gentlemen are Colonel Fitzwilliam and Mr. Darcy."

"Lizzy," asked Andrew, "can I let go of your hand now? We are almost in the park."

"Now, Andrew, did you not specifically say you would escort me to the park? I am not at the park yet," said Elizabeth smiling gently at the boy.

"Yes, Lizzy," his shoulders drooped just a bit in disappointment, "and a gentleman always keeps his word."

"Exactly," replied Elizabeth. "However, as soon

as we are at the gates you may run to your heart's content, as long as you stay where one of us adults can see you."

Andrew smiled and gave Elizabeth's hand a tug as he tried to rush her to the entrance of the park. Elizabeth laughed and walked a bit faster. At the gate, she put Michael on the ground, and Andrew dropping her hand ran about with his arms outstretched pretending to be a bird.

"He's a lively one, is he not?" she said to no one in particular, her eyes following him in his flight.

"Yes, he is." Darcy chuckled softly. "I can remember playing that game."

"Me, too," said Elizabeth. "He is learning to be a gentleman these days. Aunt Gardiner says he heard someone talking about first sons about a month ago and has since dedicated himself to taking care of his sisters and becoming a gentleman. He has his father's heart, always looking out for others." She sighed contentedly. "But enough of Andrew, how are you today, Mr. Darcy? Colonel? I would ask Mr. Bingley, but he appears to be quite well." Elizabeth gave a small, soft chuckle as she watched Jane and Mr. Bingley strolling down the path, arm in arm.

"I cannot speak for Darcy, but I am very well today, Miss Elizabeth."

"I, too, am well today. Thank you." Darcy said.

"Miss Elizabeth," began Colonel Fitzwilliam. "I am sure that my cousin is going to tell me I am too curious for my own good and call me impertinent, but you muttered something in the coffee shop yesterday that is giving my mind no rest. You mentioned that you were not going home until your mother forgave you."

"Impertinence is not something I am in the position to condemn as it seems to be a vice I struggle with as well. What I said about not going home until I am forgiven may not be completely true. I do believe my father expects me to return by Christmas at the latest, with or without my mother's forgiveness." She smiled archly at the Colonel. "Now, Colonel, what could a lady such as myself have done to warrant such censure from her mother? Is that the question that has been making your mind uneasy?"

"Indeed it is."

"And what if I told you that I could not possibly be expected to share such secrets?" She tilted her head and arched an eyebrow at Richard.

"Well, then, I suppose I would have to conjure up all sorts of possibilities. And if they are of such a secretive nature, I am afraid that your reputation, in my mind, is well and truly ruined."

"Now, Colonel, before you go conjuring, let me assure you that it is nothing so heinous as to ruin my reputation in imagination or reality. But, it is enough to make a marriage-minded mama such as mine use words to scold me such as "selfish, ungrateful, obstinate and headstrong." Does that help you figure it out, sir?"

The Colonel paced for a bit, then snapped his fingers. "You turned down an advantageous marriage proposal. Am I right?"

"You are very good, Colonel. That is it precisely. I suppose you would like the whole story, would you not? Mr. Darcy, how about you? Would you like to hear the tale?"

"I have to admit that you do have me curious," said Darcy. "But, I would not dream of forcing a confidence against your will."

"No, I suppose you know enough of my character to know that I do not respond well to being forced to do anything. That fact, however, has not become apparent to my mother. Thankfully, my father understands." Elizabeth's eyes twinkled. "Luckily for your cousin, who I suspect will either burst from curiosity or resort to all manner of interrogation methods to extract the tale, I am willing to divulge my secret." Do you remember Mr. Collins, Mr. Darcy?"

"How could one forget Mr. Collins?"

"How indeed!" agreed Elizabeth emphatically. "Following your aunt's advice, he came to Hertfordshire to find a wife. He intended to ask one of his cousins since Longbourn is entailed to him. He and your aunt thought this would be a fine olive branch to offer in order to repair a long-standing rift between his late father and my father.

"At first, he selected Jane, but seeing as she seemed to have an attachment elsewhere, he decided I might suit just as well." She smiled at the soft snort of disgust from Darcy. "So, he asked me to marry him, and I refused over and over and over again, but it was not until my mother started lecturing me about being selfish and headstrong that he decided I would not be the sort of wife of whom his patroness would approve. Mother tried to get Father to force me to accept him, but like I said, my father knows me well and would never force such an arrangement on me, entail or no entail.

"So, I am here until my mother makes peace with my decision or, as my father says, I find someone more agreeable to marry, which according to my mother is impossible since Mr. Collins was my only hope of an offer. After all, who would marry such a girl?" Elizabeth laughed.

"Who indeed?" The Colonel smirked. "Pray tell, why did you so soundly refuse this gentleman?"

"He is the most odious person I have ever met—and..." Her voice lowered to a whisper. "I have met Miss Bingley."

Richard laughed loudly. "Can he be that bad?"

"Richard, he thinks Lady Catherine can do no wrong," said Darcy.

"Oh, that is bad," said Richard with wide eyes.

"My Lizzy?" Andrew looked directly at Mr. Darcy and then placed himself between the man and his favourite cousin. "Michael threw mud at me. Can you help me get it off my face? It is cold."

She looked at Andrew. Mud was smeared across his cheek and splattered on his jacket. She crouched down to be on his level and gently wiped the mud away with her handkerchief.

"Thank you, my Lizzy." With a glance at Mr. Darcy, Andrew gave Lizzy a kiss on the cheek. "I can kiss her because I am only a young gentleman, and she is my cousin," he explained to Colonel Fitzwilliam.

Lizzy was about to stand when a small bundle came hurtling at her. "Glub, glub, glub," said Michael as he threw himself at Elizabeth.

Elizabeth expelled the air in her lungs quickly as his weight knocked her off balance and made her sit down on the ground with a thud—Michael in her lap.

"Glub, glub, glub," repeated Michael holding up a glove in his muddy hand.

"Michael, you must be more careful. Someone could get hurt," scolded Elizabeth. "Mud is not for throwing at your brother," she continued as she wiped his hand with her handkerchief and then helped him get his glove back on. "Do boys who throw mud get treats?"

Michael's eyes got big, and he shook his head slowly.

"And would you like a treat?"

Michael smiled, his head bobbing up and down.

"Then, you will keep your gloves on, and you will not throw mud," said Elizabeth firmly. "Now off with you. I will come make a boat with you in a few minutes, and we can set them floating before we go home."

"Allow me to assist you, Miss Elizabeth," said Mr. Darcy extending his hand to help her up.

"Thank you, sir." She took his hand, and he lifted her to her feet. She blushed as she checked her hair and straightened her skirts.

Darcy looked at her with a hint of laughter playing at the corners of his mouth. "You seem to have a little something here," he said tapping his nose.

Elizabeth put her hand up to her nose and felt the mud. "Oh, dear, I believe my handkerchief is of no use. Might I borrow yours, sir?" she asked, her face flushed with embarrassment.

Mr. Darcy took out his handkerchief and gently wiped the mud off the tip of her nose before taking her hand and cleaning it as well. "There, good as new," he said returning his handkerchief to his pocket.

Elizabeth smiled at Darcy in appreciation.

"I am going to go make boats," said Richard. "Maybe when you two are done there, you can join us? But, I would suggest Darcy that you steer clear of Master Andrew, or he may be calling you out for interfering with his Lizzy." Richard laughed at the matching scowls that were aimed at him and walked away toward the river.

"I suppose we should join him," said Elizabeth.

"May I escort you?" asked Darcy extending his arm.

She placed her hand on his arm and looked up at him with laughing eyes. "You might wish to take care, Mr. Darcy. Andrew is quite a possessive young man, and he will not be pleased to see another gentleman doing what he thinks is his responsibility. However, as long as your cousin does not inform him about what it means to call someone out, you might be safe."

Darcy laughed. "I did notice how he singled me out when he thought I had gotten too close to you before. I will only escort you to the boat making, and then I shall step away." He lowered his voice and whispered, "At least for now, Miss Elizabeth."

"Why Mr. Darcy," she said, colour staining her cheeks, "are you flirting with me, sir?"

"I believe I am, Miss Elizabeth. Does that bother you?"

"Not in the least. In fact, I think I rather enjoy it." She gave him a parting smile as she let go of his arm and walked over to where Andrew was busy building a boat with Colonel Fitzwilliam. "Come along, Mr. Darcy, " she called. "Everyone has to make a boat, and Michael always needs help with his. Just stay clear of the mud, we are almost out of handkerchiefs."

Darcy smiled and followed. Michael sat next to Elizabeth waving twigs and leaves in front of her.

"May I help you, Master Michael?" asked Darcy taking a seat on the ground.

Michael's eyes grew wide in awe, and he handed him the twigs and leaves. Darcy began tearing thin strips of bark off the twig explaining to Michael what he was doing with each step. Michael put his little hand on Mr. Darcy's big one so he could help tear the strips. Then, when it was time to assemble the boat, Michael climbed into Mr. Darcy's lap and helped hold the sticks and make the knots. Elizabeth watched in amazement. Her eyes were soft and a small smile graced her lips.

Richard noticed the look on Elizabeth's face and nudged Bingley who was seated next to him. He motioned toward Elizabeth and whispered, "For future reference, Bingley, it seems to work both ways."

Chapter 4

Two days later, Elizabeth and Jane waited in the sitting room for the arrival of Charlotte and Maria Lucas.

"Charlotte must be shopping for dresses." Jane speculated as she looked out the window again. "Or perhaps a new hat?"

Elizabeth gasped in horror, "Oh, Jane, you do not suppose Mr. Collins...." She could not bring herself to say it.

Jane's hand flew to her mouth, and her eyes grew wide. "No, Lizzy, she would not. Would she?"

"I truly hope she has not accepted Mr. Collins, but Charlotte is not a romantic and has only ever wanted a secure position and a modest home."

When the carriage containing Charlotte and Maria finally arrived, Elizabeth and Jane were relieved to hear that the sisters were merely in town to do some shopping and to order gowns for the Twelfth Night Assembly.

"Oh, Charlotte, we were so afraid that you had accepted Mr. Collins," said Elizabeth.

"No, Mama was afraid Mr. Collins had set his cap for Charlotte, and that is why she sent us to town," said Maria. "Last I heard, your mother was singing Mary's praises to Mr. Collins, and Mary seemed to be encouraging her."

"Mary?" said both Jane and Elizabeth.

"Consider her interests." Charlotte began enumerating them. "The pianoforte, singing, reading sermons, moralizing to everyone about everything — they might actually make a good match."

"I cannot imagine anyone with our cousin, but what you have said does make sense," admitted Elizabeth. "What other news have you from home?"

Charlotte's visage became grave. "I will tell you, but prepare yourself for a shock. In fact, I have been instructed by your father and mine to share it with not just you and Jane, but also your aunt, your uncle, and Mr. Darcy."

"Mr. Darcy?" exclaimed Elizabeth.

"Yes, it is most important that he hear this. Do you know how we might contact him?"

"That shall not be hard, Charlotte. He will be calling on Lizzy this very afternoon. He has been calling every day since we arrived. Although I must own that the first meeting was only accidental and then the second was arranged by his cousin, Colonel Fitzwilliam, but the last two days were all his own idea." Jane smiled at Elizabeth's blush. "I believe the Colonel, Mr. Bingley, and Miss Darcy will join him today."

"I told you he liked you." Charlotte gave Elizabeth a happy embrace.

"Yes, you, Jane, and my aunt," said Elizabeth. "Everyone seemed to know but me."

"Not just you, Elizabeth. Mr. Bingley said that he and Colonel Fitzwilliam had to push Mr. Darcy to admit he admired you. Never have I met a couple so right for each other, Charlotte, and yet so stubborn that they will not admit they like each other. It is the most peculiar thing."

"Most peculiar." Mrs. Gardiner gave a small laugh at Elizabeth's scowl. "I am so glad to see you have arrived safely, my dears." She gave both Charlotte and Maria a welcoming embrace. "Miss Maria,

I do believe you become more and more the image of your mother each time I see you."

Maria blushed at the compliment. "Thank you for allowing us to stay with you, Mrs. Gardiner."

"It is no trouble at all," Mrs. Gardiner assured her. "I enjoy having so many young ladies about for company." She looked at Charlotte. "Now, I have had your things taken to your room — the same one as you had on your last visit. Would you prefer to freshen up or have tea first?"

Charlotte cast an uneasy glance at her sister. "As much as I would love to freshen up before tea, we have some news of an urgent and serious nature that cannot wait for such luxuries; I am afraid. I need to share it with you, your husband and Mr. Darcy. It relates to Mr. Wickham."

Aunt Gardiner gasped as she sat heavily in a chair. "Wickham?"

"Yes." Charlotte seated herself next to Mrs. Gardiner and took the lady's hand. "I believe your husband sent a letter to Mr. Bennet regarding Mr. Wickham and warning him to keep his daughters away from the man." Mrs. Gardiner nodded. "Mr. Bennet took the letter very seriously and shared the information with my father, his closest friend.

He told no one else." Charlotte looked at Jane and Elizabeth and gave them a small but knowing smile. "Lydia was not happy with her father when he refused to allow her to visit with the officers. She spoke loudly of how unfair it was that her father would not let her see the officers and how it was her uncle from town who was a friend of Mr. Darcy's who was to blame. She spoke in great detail about the unjustness of the situation and shared her speculations about why Mr. Darcy would be so set against particular officers. She said all this while shopping one day with Maria, which is how I know it was said."

"Mr. Wickham was in the store." Maria's voice trembled. "The look on his face upon hearing Lydia was frightening. I told my father about it as soon as I got home."

Charlotte placed an arm around her sister's shoulders and drew her close. "That was in the morning three days ago. No one has seen Mr. Wickham since."

Aunt Gardiner's face was ashen. She rose and paced the room. "Roberts," she called to the butler. "Please send someone to Mr. Gardiner's office and tell him he is needed at home as soon as possible."

"Yes, ma'am," Roberts bowed and went to find a messenger.

"Elizabeth, is Mr. Darcy calling this afternoon?"

"Yes, Aunt. He, his cousin, his sister and Mr. Bingley are calling. They should be here at any moment actually."

"His sister? Oh, dear." Mrs. Gardiner sat down once again and waved her handkerchief in front of her face.

"Aunt, is there anything we can do?" asked Elizabeth. "Would you like some wine?"

Mrs. Gardiner's hand stilled, and her eyes regained their focus. "Yes, I believe I shall have a small glass. In fact, I shall set up some wine and port for our visit this afternoon as more than I shall need it." With that she hurried out of the room to arrange for refreshments and wait for her husband

~*~*~*~*~*~

It was the four young ladies from Meryton that greeted their callers.

"Miss Lucas, Miss Maria, it is good to see you again," said Bingley in his regular jovial fashion. "You know Darcy, but let me introduce you to his cousin, Colonel Fitzwilliam, and his sister, Miss

Darcy. Miss Darcy, Richard, this is Miss Lucas and her sister Miss Maria from Meryton."

"What brings you to town, Miss Lucas?" asked Mr. Darcy.

"You have not angered your mother by refusing a proposal have you?" Richard winked at Elizabeth.

"No, sir. But to be truthful, avoidance of a proposal from that very gentleman is one of the reasons my mother has shifted me to the Gardiners," Charlotte said with a laugh.

Elizabeth laughed at the Colonel's stunned expression. "Currently, he is considering my younger sister Mary. Perhaps my mother will be forgiving me sooner, rather than later."

"Oh, I hope it is not too soon. We have been enjoying your company, Miss Elizabeth," said Bingley.

"Have no fear, Mr. Bingley. Neither Jane nor I intend to run back to Meryton."

The group was just settling into conversation when the Gardiners appeared. After making the appropriate introductions and polite greetings, Mr. Gardiner took a seat and motioned for his wife to lead the conversation.

Mrs. Gardiner gave her husband's hand a small

squeeze and then remained holding it. "Gentle-men, Miss Darcy, an account has reached us from Meryton of a very unsettling nature. Due to this news, which the Miss Lucases have been instructed to share with not only Mr. Gardiner and me, but also you, Mr. Darcy, I fear our visit this afternoon will not be a pleasant one." She released her husband's hand and nodded toward the wine she had set out. He gave a slight nod of acknowl-edgment and rose to begin pouring.

"When Jane and Elizabeth first arrived, they, in the course of our conversation, mentioned that a Mr. Wickham had been stationed in Meryton. Because of my family's dealings with that man, I immediately had my husband write to Mr. Bennet warning him to keep his daughters away from Mr. Wickham. Thankfully, he received the news with the gravity it required and put measures in place in an attempt to protect his daughters." Mrs. Gar-diner accepted a glass of wine from her husband.

"Your family has had dealing with Mr. Wick-ham?" Richard asked. "They must have been of a serious nature to prompt such immediate action on the part of both your husband and Mr. Bennet?"

Mrs. Gardiner nodded. "Indeed, they were, but

I will get to my family's story in a moment. First, I would like to have Miss Lucas share what she told me earlier about an incident in Meryton."

Elizabeth noted the exchange of hard looks that passed between Darcy and Richard as Charlotte repeated what had happened at the store, pausing to allow Maria to speak of seeing Mr. Wickham in the store.

"And no one has seen him for three days?" asked Richard.

"That is correct," said Charlotte.

"And you believe he may come to town to see Darcy because a young girl has been denied his company and he believes Darcy is spreading tales about him?"

"Yes, in a matter of speaking, I suppose you could state it that way, Colonel," said Mr. Gardiner. "However, our concerns go further than that. Our nieces are known to both Mr. Darcy and Mr. Wickham."

"Mr. Wickham knew of Jane and Elizabeth visiting their uncle. Had he not known, Lydia's complaining would have alerted him to that fact." Charlotte looked to Mrs. Gardiner and then Elizabeth. "She did not just mention Mr. Darcy's name.

She also mentioned Elizabeth and said she did not see how Lizzy could abide being friends with such an unpleasant gentleman."

This information brought a greater understanding of the situation not only to the gentlemen but also to Elizabeth. "You...you fear for our safety, Uncle?"

"We do."

"And your dealings with him, Mrs. Gardiner?" Richard leaned forward in his chair.

"I had a niece named Elise Cooke. She was the daughter of my eldest sister." She turned to Mr. Darcy. "You may remember her. She was fortunate to gain a position caring for your mother during her illness."

Darcy's brows furrowed. "I believe I do remember her. She was very kind to both Georgiana and me. She actually spoke to me when I asked her about my mother. And she comforted my sister with songs and stories on many occasions."

Mrs. Gardiner smiled sadly. "Elise found her duties well-suited to her generous and gentle nature. It was that nature combined with her beauty which drew young men to seek her attention. One of those young men was Mr. Wickham."

Darcy's face blanched and dread gripped his heart. Wickham and young maids had never been a good combination.

"But, Elise knew of Mr. Wickham's reputation. She had been warned both of his habits and his charm. As a result, when he tried to draw her into conversation, she was civil but did not allow herself to be taken in by his pleasing manners and his smooth tongue. However, instead of being put off by her dismissals, he seemed to find them a challenge to be overcome." She paused and darted a quick glance at her husband who nodded his encouragement. "I am aware that the remainder of my tale is truly not fit for maidenly ears, and it is not my wish to be indelicate. I will not excuse my nieces from this discussion, but I would understand if Miss Darcy or Miss Maria were to be asked to leave the room. There are many books, even a few novels, in my husband's study that might be entertaining." She lifted an impertinent eyebrow and smiled at the two young girls before directing a questioning look to both Charlotte and Darcy.

Charlotte shook her head. "Maria already knows the content of your letter to Mr. Bennet."

Darcy looked at his sister. He knew she was far

better acquainted with the devious nature of a man such as Wickham than most girls her age. "Do you wish to remain?" he asked.

"I will stay," said Georgiana softly.

"Very well," said Mrs. Gardiner. "Your talks with my niece, Mr. Darcy, did not go unnoticed by Mr. Wickham. He questioned her about them and refused to believe they were as she said, mere inquiries into the wellbeing of Mrs. Darcy. His attentions to her increased. He said hateful things about you, Mr. Darcy. Things she would not repeat. But in her opinion, he possessed a greedy and jealous heart, a heart which desired to have all that you possessed." She paused and drew a deep breath. Mr. Gardiner took her hand and held it firmly. "However, his heart was darker than she could have ever imagined, for he sought an opportunity to ruin her and forced himself upon her, threatening to harm her should she ever tell anyone about it. She, of course, was frightened and understandably ashamed. She wrote to me of it only when she needed my help to tell her mother she was with child."

Mr. Gardiner placed his handkerchief in her hand. "She was sent to us," he continued. "She arrived as Elise Monahan, a young widow whose husband had been tragically killed in an accident. We had means to help her establish herself after the baby was born, but sadly our assistance was never needed as both she and the baby died in childbirth two days before her nineteenth birthday."

"She did not leave to care for an ailing relative?" asked Darcy breaking the silence which had engulfed the room.

Mrs. Gardiner shook her head.

"She was harmed in an attempt to harm me?" There was great sadness in his voice.

"Something for which you are not responsible," said Richard firmly.

"He is right, Mr. Darcy." Mr. Gardiner held Darcy's gaze for a moment. "We can only be held responsible for our actions, not those of others."

Mrs. Gardiner spoke softly. "I know from the stories I heard while I was living in Lambton that Mr. Wickham tormented you. He seemed bent on making you suffer for having been born to your status. I know that each time, his attacks became more personal, closer to home. Though he will not attack you personally; he seems rather determined to make you suffer. I do not know how he has treated you since your father died, but I imagine, his attacks are not any less personal."

Darcy nodded. "You would be correct."

"His last attack on my brother was very close to home," said Georgiana.

"Georgiana," cautioned Darcy.

"No, brother, "said Georgiana. "I must be allowed to speak of it." She waited until Darcy gave a resigned nod. "Last summer, Mr. Wickham convinced me to elope with him. I was foolish." Her cheeks grew rosy, and she looked at her hands which were folded in her lap. "I was taken with his looks and manners. He was all that was pleasing, just as a young man should be. He spoke so eloquently of his feelings for me that I believed he really loved me. Before we were to elope, I thought better of my plans and wished to be allowed to tell my brother of my desire to wed. Mr. Wickham became incensed. He berated me for being so inconstant in my feelings and childlike in my behaviour. He accused me of playing him false and threatened to tell my brother I had allowed him liberties."

She looked to her brother. "I later discovered

he was only after two things, my dowry and my brother. Had I followed through with the elopement, his revenge would have been complete. Fitzwilliam would have suffered severely for the rest of his life, I know this now." She finished in a small voice that was filled with sorrow.

"Mr. Gardiner," said Roberts coming into the room. "A Lieutenant Saunderson to see you, sir."

"Send him in, Roberts. What he has to say may be shared with all who are here."

"Lieutenant," Mr. Gardiner rose to greet the officer and introduced him to the others in the room. "I assume you bear news from Meryton?"

"Yes, sir. Colonel Forster sent me, sir." He glanced nervously toward the ladies. "It is about Lieutenant Wickham, sir."

"I expected as much. Please continue."

"Very good, sir. Colonel Forster wished me to inform you that Lieutenant Wickham was spotted in town two days ago. According to a witness we have recently located, he asked some people at the park about a lovely family that was playing near the water. The family consisted of three gentlemen, two ladies, and four children. Upon further questioning, we were made aware that one of the gentlemen was Mr. Darcy and another was Colonel Fitzwilliam. Colonel Forester immediately wished me to inform both you and Mr. Darcy. Would I be correct in informing Colonel Forster that the others of the family are members of your household, sir?"

"You would be correct. I suspect Colonel Forster had already come to that conclusion?"

Lieutenant Saunderson nodded. "Indeed he had."

"You may report the following to him. No one will be leaving this house without an escort. You must have a footman or one of these gentlemen with you at all times when you are out and about. This applies to all of you ladies and my children as well, but I think we know that, Lizzy, this is most particularly important for you. Wickham befriended you in Meryton and has now seen you in the company of Mr. Darcy. If his pattern holds, you would be his first choice as a target. I hate to be so blunt, but I would rather be blunt than to have you injured or worse, Lizzy."

"Of course, Uncle. I will be very cautious," replied a shaken Elizabeth.

Darcy's heart ached as he saw the fear in her

eyes. Silently, he cursed George Wickham and vowed that this would be the last time Wickham would trouble his family. His mind caught on the word. He looked about the room. Yes, the word was correct. These people would hopefully soon be his family.

Chapter 5

At the Gardiner house, the shock of the news concerning Wickham gradually wore off, and the awkwardness of the recently imposed safety precautions melted into a sort of routine. One week later, the entire household, save Mr. Gardiner, who was at work and Michael, who was too young, prepared for a gift buying excursion.

"John," said Mrs. Gardiner, "We shall be ready to depart in half an hour."

"Thank you, ma'am. I will be ready," replied the burly footman.

Half an hour later, true to her word, Mrs. Gardiner had the entire party gathered at the front door, ready to depart. "It will be a bit of a squeeze getting us all in the carriage," she said, "but we shan't catch a chill being so cozy together, now shall we?" She let Charlotte, Maria, Elizabeth and

Jane climb into the carriage first before handing in her three children and instructing them to sit on a lap or squish tighter. Then she climbed in, and John joined the driver on the box.

"Mama?" asked Andrew. "May we stop for Papa's book first?"

"Yes, Andrew, I think we shall," she told him. Then turning to Elizabeth, she added merrily, "I dare say if it is not the first stop, we shall hear of little else all morning."

Elizabeth winked at her aunt and wrapped her arms more tightly around the youngster who sat on her lap. "It is the best shop, is it not, Andrew?"

Andrew scrunched up his face as he thought for a moment before giving a small shake of his head. "It is almost the best. The sweets shop is better." A smile split his face at the thought of the treats contained within that shop.

Mrs. Gardiner chuckled. "I know of a lovely tea shop with chocolate and scones just down the street from the bookseller's."

"Oh, yes," said Jane. "Their chocolate was delightful."

"And the company may be just as pleasing." Mrs. Gardiner's eyes sparkled with mischief. "The gentlemen did say they frequent that shop, did they not?"

"They did," answered Elizabeth.

Andrew peeked up at his favourite cousin and pulled his brows together which combined with his slight pout let everyone know he was not best pleased with this information. "Will Mr. Darcy be there?" he asked.

A faint blush coloured Elizabeth's cheeks. She hoped he would be. At the end of each year, it was Gardiner tradition to give gifts that showed thankfulness for and gave blessing to the receiver. Although she enjoyed spending time searching for just the right gift, she had been disappointed she would not be home to receive a call from Darcy and Georgiana. "Perhaps."

Andrew's expression became more of a scowl. "Colonel Fitzwilliam, too?"

Elizabeth nodded.

Andrew's face relaxed somewhat although he still did not look satisfied. "I like chocolate," he said. He worried his bottom lip for a moment as he thought before he sighed. "But I think I still prefer the sweets shop."

The carriage groaned to a stop outside the bookseller.

John jumped down from the box and went into the store. A short while later, he opened the carriage door and handed the ladies and children down. Then, after a quick word with Mrs. Gardiner, he took up his post at the front door, carefully watching each person who entered.

Margaret, Amelia, and Andrew followed their mother first to the section of books from which to choose a present for their father. After making their selection, they waited near the children's books while Mrs. Gardiner picked up a few other books, carefully hiding them from Elizabeth's view and paid for them. Elizabeth had already made her purchase and was wandering the shop admiring the row on row of books. She stopped at a shelf of poetry books and paged through a few.

"Lizzy," said Andrew tugging at her coat, "it's time to go."

Elizabeth took his hand and walked to the front of the store. "Oh, dear," she said.

"Is there a problem?" asked her aunt.

"I seem to have left my parcel back on the shelf by the poetry books. It will only take a moment to retrieve it." She turned back into the store as the rest of the group, save Andrew, who was still holding her hand, chatted on the walkway out front.

"Excuse me, sir. I left my parcel on the shelf," she said to a gentleman in great coat and top hat who was perusing the same volume of poetry that she had previously been enjoying.

"Ah, Miss Elizabeth," said the man turning to face her. "It is a pleasure to see you again."

Elizabeth gasped and jumped back, pushing Andrew behind her. "Mr. Wickham, are you on leave from the regiment?" She hoped her voice sounded steadier than she felt.

"You could say that," he said with a smirk. "I am on a sort of mission, I guess."

"It would be a pity to keep you from your purpose, and my party is waiting for me, so I will wish you a good day, Mr. Wickham." She gave a quick curtsey and began backing away from him.

"Miss Elizabeth, your leaving would keep me from my mission," he said taking a step closer and pulling a pistol out of his pocket. "I would suggest that you stop." A menacing sneer suffused his face.

Elizabeth froze. Keeping her eyes fixed on

Wickham's face, she gave Andrew a little push towards the door and hissed, "Run!"

Wickham's eyes flicked toward the young boy, his pistol following his gaze. In desperation, Elizabeth threw her package at the gun and lunged toward her cousin. A gunshot reverberated through the store.

Mrs. Gardiner's eyes grew wide in terror. "Jane, get the girls in the carriage. Someone get help." She ran after John, who had already entered the store.

Maria lifted her skirts and raced down the street toward a group of men who stood chatting in front of the tea shop. "Help!" she cried. "Oh, please help us!"

"What happened?" asked Richard as he caught her by the arm.

"A gunshot." She gasped trying to quickly fill her lungs with air. "At the bookstore." She again took a gasping breath. "Elizabeth and Andrew…" It was enough. Richard was running toward the book shop following closely behind his cousin while Bingley hurried behind them with Maria.

Darcy was the first to enter the store and came around the book stack only moments after Mrs. Gardiner. He froze as he took in the scene. Wickham lay motionless on the floor, a pile of books surrounding him. A gun lay several feet away from him, and John was standing over him. In front of Darcy, Elizabeth clutched the lifeless form of Andrew. Mrs. Gardiner dropped to the floor beside Elizabeth and began checking her son for injuries. There was blood, a good deal of blood.

"Aunt, take him, please." Elizabeth's words slurred, and her body swayed. "I am not feelin...." She slumped against her Aunt. It was then that Darcy realized the blood was not just from the wound on Andrew's leg but was also from a wound on Elizabeth's arm. Mrs. Gardiner lifted her son from Elizabeth's arms as Darcy lifted Elizabeth from the floor

"Bingley!" Darcy yelled. "Your cravat, give it to Mrs. Gardiner, she can use it as a bandage to stop Andrew's bleeding." He waited for Bingley to hand the piece of cloth to Mrs. Gardiner. "Now, take my cravat and tie it around Miss Elizabeth's wound. Tightly!" Bingley did as instructed. "Send Miss Bennet and the children home, then bring Gardiner's physician," he looked to Mrs. Gardiner for the name.

"Dr. Clarke, the same one who attended your father," Mrs. Gardiner said looking at Bingley.

"Bring Dr. Clarke to Gracechurch Street as quickly as possible. And my carriage —send it round back of the store."

"And a surgeon," added Richard. "We will need a surgeon to close those wounds."

Bingley shook his head. "Dr. Clarke still has his apprentice, does he not, Mrs. Gardiner?"

"He does indeed." She stroked her son's hair as a tear slid down her cheek. "Andrew knows him. It will make it easier."

"I will make haste," Bingley assured Mrs. Gardiner before turning to do as he had been instructed.

"Colonel, you will come to the Gardiner's once that," Darcy indicated Wickham with a tilt of his head in the man's direction, "has been disposed of."

Richard nodded. "John and I will move him to new accommodations as soon as you have removed the injured."

"Sir," Darcy addressed the shopkeeper who had come running from the back of the store and stood wringing his hands and staring at the scene before him, "where is your back door? We mustn't exit to the street." The man's eyes shifted to Darcy. "You will want to lock the front door and hang up your sign. I am afraid the shop is not fit for customers at the moment."

"Yes, sir." The shopkeeper immediately locked his door and then returned. "Follow me, sir. The backdoor is just through here."

"Mrs. Gardiner, are you well enough to carry Andrew?" Darcy asked in a gentle voice.

She nodded. "I will follow you."

Darcy carefully positioned Elizabeth in the carriage and then took Andrew from Mrs. Gardiner as she climbed in. He placed the boy back in his mother's arms, and after giving directions to his driver and sending one of his footmen to Mr. Gardiner's warehouse, he climbed in next to Elizabeth's still form and gathered her into his arms. It would not do to have her jostled about by the motion of the carriage.

Mrs. Gardiner gave him a half smile. "They will be well." Her voice wavered.

"Yes, of course, they will be well." Darcy swallowed the lump that rose in his throat. "They must be well," he whispered.

~*~*~*~*~*~

The doctor arrived shortly after Mrs. Gardiner, Jane, and Charlotte had, with the help of Mr. Darcy, gotten Andrew and Elizabeth into bed. Darcy paced the sitting room while he and Bingley waited for news.

Mr. Gardiner burst into the house, hat in hand, coat unbuttoned. "Roberts, tell me what is happening."

"Mr. Bingley and Mr. Darcy are in the sitting room, and Dr. Clarke is attending Miss Elizabeth and Master Andrew, sir,"

"Wickham?" Mr. Gardiner asked as he entered the sitting room.

"He was at the book shop," said Darcy.

"Whose...?" Mr. Gardiner sat heavily in his chair, his eyes resting on the blood-stained coat which lay discarded on a footstool.

"Elizabeth's and Andrew's," replied Darcy coming to a stop in front of him. "I do not know the details, but both have sustained wounds from a gunshot. The doctor is with them now. We are just waiting for word."

"Wickham has been taken into custody," added Bingley.

"He will not be hurting anyone again," said Richard coming into the room. "He was conscious when we took him in, and we got his statement—with a little coercing." He smiled wickedly. "Of course, I will need to talk to Miss Elizabeth and Andrew later to confirm the veracity of his words. However," he rubbed his fist, "I have little reason to believe he was anything less than honest."

Richard took Darcy by the shoulders and steered him to a chair. "Sit. Your constant pacing does no one any good. It only stirs up the nerves."

Darcy acquiesced and took a seat. "What can you tell us about what happened?"

Richard unbuttoned his jacket before sitting down. "It is quite a tale if it is true." He tossed one leg over the other and settled back to share his story. "Wickham says he saw the footman at the front of the store, so he slipped in through the back door. He confronted Miss Elizabeth when she came back into the store to retrieve a forgotten parcel. He claims he brandished the gun to intimidate Miss Elizabeth and make her follow him out of the store to the alley. Apparently, Miss Elizabeth is not easily intimidated."

Mr. Gardiner snorted. "Indeed she is not."

Richard chuckled. "Instead of cowering in fear, she told Andrew to run for help. That is when Wickham took a shot at your son, Mr. Gardiner. However, his efforts were somewhat thwarted by Miss Elizabeth, who concurrently stepped in front of the gun and threw an object knocking the gun out of his hand, but not until the shot had been fired.

"Wickham asserts that Andrew stumbled and fell, hitting his head rendering him insensible. At this point, Miss Elizabeth rounded on Wickham and showered him with books before pummeling him senseless with an exceptionally large volume of poetry."

All three men sat slack-jawed listening to the Colonel's recital of the events that had occurred in the book shop.

Richard gave his cousin a sympathetic smile. "He admitted he was only after Miss Elizabeth to make you suffer."

"Elizabeth beat Wickham?" asked Mr. Gardiner incredulously.

"With a very large book of poetry," said Richard.

"I always knew she had a temper, and she has

always said her courage rises at every attempt to intimidate, but you have to admit, that is impressive," said Mr. Gardiner. "She really stepped in front of a gun to save my son?"

"It appears so. By throwing her parcel at Wickham and distracting him by moving, the bullet went wild. I shudder to think of the results if it had not."

"As do I," said a distinguished looking gentleman as he entered the room. "Mr. Thompson is nearly finished with the closures of the wounds which have been thoroughly cleaned and will be well-dressed by Miss Lucas. She is quite knowledgeable concerning wounds and the prevention of infection. She says it comes from having two younger brothers." The gentleman greeted Bingley and then introduced himself to Darcy before continuing. "The bullet only grazed both Master Gardiner and Miss Elizabeth, although it appears to have nicked a bone in Miss Elizabeth's arm," said Dr. Clarke. "The quick thinking in tying off the injuries, Mr. Darcy, to prevent blood loss was most beneficial. I am convinced my assessment would not have been so positive if any more blood had been lost." He gave an appreciative bow of his head to Darcy.

"They will both need to remain calm for a few days while the stitches take, and Miss Elizabeth's arm will need to be kept in a sling for at least two weeks to restrict use in order for the bone to have time to heal. As I said, Miss Lucas seems to be quite capable of tending the wounds properly, but Mr. Thompson will, of course, return on the morrow to check on the patients." He donned his jacket and straightened his waistcoat. "Master Gardiner suffered a blow to the head that will give him a headache for a while but will not put him in danger or be of lasting consequence.

"I am not sure which patient will be the hardest to restrain," the doctor said with a grin that caused the skin of his face to crinkle, "but I have a feeling it will not be the young master." He took his hat from Roberts, placed it atop his grey head and tucked his walking stick under his arm. "I have left some draughts for pain and sleep with Mrs. Gardiner should they be needed. Again," he chuckled softly, "administering them may be a challenge, knowing from experience a certain young lady's dislike of medicine." He shook the hand Mr. Gardiner had extended to him. "Do not hesitate to send for me if the condition of either changes." He picked up his bag.

"Are we ready, Mr. Thompson?" he questioned the younger man who had just entered the room.

"Yes, sir, we are."

"Then I will wish you a good day, Mr. Gardiner, gentlemen." He gave a final bow and took his leave.

Mr. Gardiner sighed in relief. "I think I shall go up and see the patients. Would you gentlemen care to join me?"

~*~*~*~*~*~

"Thank you, Elizabeth, for protecting Andrew," said Mr. Gardiner softly as he gave his niece a kiss on the forehead. "We wanted to see with our own eyes that you were well," he said more loudly. "We shall leave you to rest, and to help you rest most easy, I want you to know that Wickham is in custody and poses a threat to no one. Tomorrow, the Colonel will be back to ask you some questions to verify Wickham's statements."

"But, I could answer them now," protested Elizabeth weakly.

"No, tomorrow," said her uncle. "The doctor's orders are to rest. Tomorrow will be soon enough."

Each gentleman in turn stepped forward and gave their wishes for a speedy recovery, and then turned to go. Darcy was the last to give his well wishes. As he turned to leave, Elizabeth called him back.

"Mr. Darcy, I want to thank you for helping us. The doctor said the bandages probably saved our lives. I believe I owe you a new cravat," she said with a slight teasing tone.

Darcy took a seat in the chair next to her bed and looked around the room. The others had proceeded to Andrew's room ahead of him, leaving him alone with Elizabeth.

"You gave me quite a scare, Elizabeth," he said gravely. "I am glad we—I—did not lose you today."

Elizabeth smiled at his familiar address. The look in his eyes left no doubt in her mind that he held her dear. She blinked away the tears this realization brought to her eyes and placed her hand on his.

"Please be a good patient, Elizabeth. I could not bear to have you unwell for long. Take the medicine and rest. I will see you tomorrow." He grasped her hand in his and gave it a small squeeze before leaving the room.

In the next room, Andrew lay quietly on his bed. His father, Bingley and Colonel Fitzwilliam had already given him their well wishes.

"Papa?" said Andrew when he saw Darcy. "Might Mr. Darcy stay with me a while?"

Mr. Gardiner gave his son a puzzled look. "Of course, if you wish and Mr. Darcy is agreeable."

"I would be honoured to spend some time with you, Master Andrew," Darcy said with a bow that made the little boy giggle.

"Fine, then we will leave you," said Mr. Gardiner. "Dinner will be in about an hour. Until then, we shall be relaxing in the parlour."

Darcy nodded his understanding and sat in the chair next to Andrew's bed. "What can I do for you, Master Andrew?" He asked.

"Mama says you helped me," the boy stated, looking inquisitively into Darcy's eyes.

"I had Mr. Bingley put a bandage on your leg, and then drove you home in my carriage," explained Darcy.

"What happened to Mr. Wickedman?" asked Andrew.

Darcy smiled at the mispronunciation of Wickham's name but thought it seemed most appropriate. He noticed how Andrew was anxiously winding his blanket around his fingers, and replied in a calming voice, "My cousin and some of his soldier friends have locked him up. He will never be able to hurt anyone again."

A smile spread across Andrew's face in relief. Then, his eyebrows drew together in a pensive look. "Did you help my Lizzy, too?"

"I did."

"A gentleman always helps others in need, right?"

"Yes."

"You are a very good gentleman, Mr. Darcy," stated Andrew.

"Thank you," said an amused Darcy. He waited as Andrew thought about something which appeared from the various expressions on the young boy's face to be very important.

"Do you love my Lizzy?" Andrew put his small hand on Mr. Darcy's arm and looked him straight in the eye. "I would like for you to love my Lizzy, Mr. Darcy, because you are a very good gentleman, and she is a lady."

Darcy smiled down at the innocent face peering up at him. "Your Lizzy is a very special lady, Master Andrew, and yes, I do love her. But, only you and I know that, so it must be our secret until I have a chance to tell her, do you understand?" Andrew nodded his head. "Telling ladies you love them is not as easy for older gentlemen as it is for younger gentlemen."

"And you must only kiss a lady when you stand under a gauge at the end of a court or something like that," said Andrew his nose wrinkled in uncertainty.

Darcy chuckled. "You mean a gentleman may kiss a lady when he is engaged or betrothed to the lady. That means he has promised to marry her. Engagement happens after a courtship." Andrew had propped himself up on his elbows and listened intently. Darcy took another pillow from the bed and placed it behind the youngster's back. "A courtship is when you call on just one special lady so that you can get to know her, and she can get to know you. Then you can see if marriage is agreeable to both the lady and the gentleman. But neither a courtship nor a marriage can happen without permission from the lady and her father or another male relative in whose care she resides."

"Oh," said Andrew, his eyebrows knit together as he pondered what he had heard. "So, you must ask my Lizzy to call on her special and if she says yes, then you have to ask my papa or her papa?"

"Yes, and then if I wanted to marry your Lizzy, I would have to ask for permission all over again."

A frown pulled at the corners of Andrew's mouth. "That is a lot of rules," he said at last. "Sometimes when I ask my papa for something I get scared he will say no. Is it scary like that for older gentlemen, too?"

"Yes, it is," said Darcy with a smile.

"But, a gentleman must be brave," Andrew said to himself. "You will ask my Lizzy and my papa, will you not?"

"Sometime, Master Andrew, sometime soon," said Darcy. "Now, if you have no further questions, I believe it is almost time for dinner, and your mama will want you to rest. I should go join your papa and the others. A gentleman must be friendly to the men before he asks for permission." Darcy gave Andrew's nose a tap.

"I think you are very friendly, Mr. Darcy," said Andrew.

Darcy smiled and stood to leave.

"Mr. Darcy?" There was a hopeful tone to the child's voice.

"Yes, Master Andrew?"

"Lizzy usually reads to me, but Mama says she cannot. Would you read me a story tonight?"

"I shall return after dinner. It would be my honour, sir." Darcy bowed his leave.

Downstairs he was met by a roomful of questioning eyes, but he just smiled and took his seat.

"You and Master Andrew spoke for a long time," commented Richard.

"Yes, we did," answered Darcy.

"And you spoke about...." prodded his cousin.

"He wanted to say thank you for helping him and Miss Elizabeth."

"And that is all?" questioned Bingley. "Surely, that did not take so long?"

"He also wanted to know what happened to Mr. Wickedman. Is that not the best name for him, Richard?" said Darcy. "I think he was nervous about Wickham being able to hurt him again."

"That is understandable," said Mr. Gardiner.

"But, I sincerely doubt it took very long to assure him of his safety."

"No, it did not take very long," said Darcy. "He had some questions regarding being a gentleman." He noted Mr. Gardiner's raised brows. "Do not worry, sir, I answered them very properly. And, Richard, Bingley, you will be happy to know that I have been declared a very good gentleman by Master Andrew."

"That is a relief, cousin," said Richard earning a laugh from Bingley. "Was there anything else?"

"Only that he made me promise to read him a story before I leave. So, I will have to skip our port after dinner, as a very good gentleman always keeps his promises." Darcy chuckled.

~*~*~*~*~*~

After her visitors had left and as she was preparing for bed, Mrs. Gardiner said, "I heard most of Mr. Darcy's conversation with Andrew before I joined you in the drawing room. "

"Eavesdropping were you, Madeline? How improper," teased Mr. Gardiner.

"I did not mean to eavesdrop. I had come up to check on both Andrew and Lizzy. I wanted to know if they needed anything. It was so sweet, dear. Mr. Darcy will make a wonderful father someday."

"Is that all you are going to tell me?"

"Well, Mr. Darcy already told you most everything."

"Most everything?"

"Yes, but the part he left out is a secret."

"Madeline, you know I do not like secrets," Mr. Gardiner said severely.

"Oh, Edward. It is nothing to be concerned about. In fact, Mr. Darcy plans to share the secret with you sometime soon." She laughed at the perplexed look on her husband's face. "Very well, but you must not let on that you know," she cautioned. "Andrew asked Mr. Darcy if he loved Lizzy. And he asked him if he was going to talk to you about a courtship—although those are not the words Andrew used."

"And?"

"And what, Mr. Gardiner?" She teased as she settled back against her pillows and opened the book she intended to read.

"And what did Mr. Darcy say?" Mr. Gardiner took her book from her and placed it well out of her reach on the other side of him.

"Mr. Darcy said yes to both questions. And our son has given him permission to love his Lizzy, so I hope that you will too when Mr. Darcy comes to you," Mrs. Gardiner said with a laugh.

"I would not dream of refusing as long as Lizzy is agreeable," said Mr. Gardiner with a grin.

"I do not think she will be disagreeable, dear." Mr. Gardiner raised his eyebrows in surprise. His wife continued as she snuggled up to his side and slid her hand in the direction of her book, "She took her medicine without complaint tonight, and when I asked her why, she said because Mr. Darcy asked her to!"

He stopped her hand and held it to his heart. "Well, I dare say we must do what we can to keep him around then, my dear—at least until the doctor says she can stop the medicine."

"I think I shall like having him for a nephew, Edward. And, I think her mother will forgive her about Mr. Collins if she brings home Mr. Darcy instead." She propped herself up to look down at him. "Now, might I have my book?"

Mr. Gardiner shook his head and moved her book to the nightstand.

~*~*~*~*~

Darcy smiled more than normal on the way home that night.

"It seems young Andrew Gardiner has had a most pleasing effect on my cousin, Bingley. He has not stopped smiling all night."

Darcy looked at Richard and taunted him by smiling even more.

"I believe he has put a spell on him, Bingley. I did not receive a scowl in return for my jibe."

"And you shan't tonight. Wickham has been captured, Elizabeth is safe, and I am a very good gentleman!" Darcy shot back.

"Ah, yes, a very good gentleman. And pray tell what makes you such a good gentleman, Darcy?" asked Richard.

"I helped Andrew and his Lizzy."

"And what has Master Andrew given you in return for your help on his behalf—aside from his ardent praise and devotion?"

"Permission."

"Permission for what?" asked Bingley.

"Permission to love his Lizzy."

Bingley and Richard laughed. "So no more standing between the two of you or taunting you by kissing her?" said Richard.

"No. I am free and clear, except I was cautioned that older gentlemen do not kiss ladies unless they are standing under a gauge at the end of a court."

"What?" Bingley and Richard said in unison.

"Understanding, engagement, courtship," explained Darcy.

"And were those the things you had to explain about gentlemen?" asked Bingley.

"Yes, those and a few other things," said Darcy. "But the rest is our secret." Darcy pretended to lock his lips and throw away the key. Then, he rested his head against the back of the carriage, closed his eyes and proceeded to ignore his companions for the remainder of the trip.

Chapter 6

"Good day, Gardiner," Lord Matlock's deep voice reverberated through the warehouse.

"Good day, Matlock. What can we do for you today?" asked Mr. Gardiner.

"Just stopped by to see about my order. I see it is being shipped as we speak. I can always count on you to get things done on time," said Lord Matlock clapping Mr. Gardiner on the back.

"Thank you, sir. But you could have sent someone to check on it." Mr. Gardiner eyed Lord Matlock suspiciously.

A laugh rumbled softly from his belly. "Never have been able to put one past you."

Mr. Gardiner took his hat and coat from the hook on his office wall. "We have callers coming to check on the invalids today, so I was just on my way home. Two of them are your relatives. If you wish to speak to me, I suggest you join me." Mr. Gardiner motioned for Lord Matlock to precede him out of the office. "I have an excellent bottle of port in my study—better than the vintage here in my office."

"I cannot pass up a bottle of port if you say it's excellent, now can I?" Lord Matlock followed Mr. Gardiner from the warehouse. "Allow me to offer my carriage as our transportation." He motioned to the fine black equipage that stood in front of the warehouse. Mr. Gardiner accepted and soon they were rolling up the street to the Gardiners' town-house.

"Richard has told me how your niece has been instrumental in removing a thorn from the side of my family," began Lord Matlock.

"Not just your family, mine as well."

Lord Matlock nodded his acknowledgement and continued, "I also understand she and your son were injured in the process. I wish to send my well wishes to your family along with my thanks. Richard has shared the story with me about how Miss Elizabeth dispatched of the scoundrel and put herself in danger to protect your son. She sounds like quite the lady."

"That she is. She is a favourite of ours at the Gardiner house. Although having her visit now that she is grown is less strenuous than it was when she was a girl." Mr. Gardiner laughed.

"Lively, was she?"

"Still is, but time and age have assisted in containing it within ladylike confines—most times. My children adore both she and her sister Jane, but Lizzy is the one who commands the brood with the efficiency of a military commander." Mr. Gardiner peered through the carriage window. "My eldest son, Andrew, is most devoted to her—she is his favourite. It is Andrew who is injured."

"She seems to be a favourite of my nephew, too. At least that is the word I get from Richard."

"Ah, so we come to it." Mr. Gardiner smiled. "Richard is not one to tell tales, my friend. I assume you are looking out for your nephew in his father's stead."

"Quite right. He is of age and does not require my approval for anything, but I would like to know what he might be getting himself into, just the same."

"Naturally. I would do the same for my niece if I

did not know your family as well as I do. The house is just here."

Lord Matlock tapped the carriage roof.

"May I suggest an introduction to Elizabeth and a brief visit with the group that has gathered before we retire to my study for some discussion?"

"And port." Lord Matlock took note of the carriage parked just up the street. "I see Darcy is here already."

"And I would assume Bingley and the Colonel are with him," said Mr. Gardiner.

"Yes, Richard told me Bingley is quite taken with your eldest niece."

"It is quite easy for many of the young men Jane meets to be taken with her. She is sweet to a fault and quite a beauty."

Mr. Gardiner and Lord Matlock handed their outerwear to Roberts.

"Father!" exclaimed Richard coming into the entryway. "What brings you to Cheapside today? Checking up on Darcy?"

"Of course," replied his father.

Richard laughed but put a hand on his father's shoulder to forestall his entry into the parlour. Leaning close, he whispered, "I must warn you, the atmosphere here is unique. The picture of familial felicity can have a peculiar effect on a person." And with that, Richard removed his hand from his father's shoulder allowing him to enter the room.

From the doorway, Lord Matlock surveyed the scene before him. Mr. Gardiner was being greeted by his daughters and wife while lively conversation flowed around the room. He saw Bingley seated next to a young lady who he assumed to be Jane Bennet. Mr. Gardiner had certainly not exaggerated about her beauty. He noted two other young ladies, who, based on information from Richard, he guessed to be the Lucas sisters from Meryton. And then there was Darcy.

"It is rather like looking into the future, is it not, Father?" said Richard softly when he heard his father draw a quick breath. His father nodded.

On the far side of the room, Darcy was seated on a settee. A dark-haired boy with a bandaged leg sat next to him while a smaller boy sat on his lap with his curly head snuggled into Darcy's shoulder. Darcy was reading a book to the boys and was being watched by a handsome young lady whose arm was in a sling. He studied her face as she laughed and conversed with those around her. Her eyes never strayed too long from his nephew, and he saw a tender smile pass between the two as Gardiner began to introduce him to the room.

"Children," said Mrs. Gardiner after the introductions were made. "It is time to return to the nursery. Mrs. Eddington will be waiting."

"Mr. Darcy?" Lord Matlock heard Andrew address his nephew. "Will you carry me to my room? Papa has been working all day and should rest."

"Certainly, Master Andrew—if your father approves." Mr. Gardiner nodded. Darcy placed Michael on the floor and scooped up Andrew.

"Mr. Darcy? I need to give my Lizzy a kiss first," said Andrew.

"As you wish," said Darcy, and he held Andrew so that he could place a kiss on Elizabeth's cheek.

"Me, too. Me, too," said Michael as he jumped up and down next to Elizabeth. Elizabeth leaned down so that he could also place a kiss on her cheek. Then catching hold of Darcy's coat, Michael followed his brother out of the room. Elizabeth smiled sweetly as she watched them walk away.

Matlock took the seat that Darcy had just vacated. "Miss Elizabeth, I want to extend my family's well wishes for your health and our thanks for your help in apprehending Wickham."

A blush coloured Elizabeth's pale cheeks. "I thank you, sir, but I did nothing more than go shopping for books. It was more of a right time, right place sort of thing," she demurred. "Or would that be the wrong time, wrong place?" she added with a laugh lifting her injured arm just a bit.

"I dare say it is not every young lady that would be quick thinking enough to use books as weapons. Another may have let Wickham get away."

"It was more a matter of making sure Andrew and I could get away," said Elizabeth gravely. "I was fortunate to have such weapons so readily available. They do say the word is mightier than the sword, and apparently it is equally as effective against pistols." She smiled.

"So, it was a lucky throw that disarmed your assailant?" asked Lord Matlock.

"Milord," said Charlotte, "there is no such thing as a lucky throw with Lizzy. Her aim is legendary in the annals of childhood battles in Hertfordshire. She is the undisputed champion of our lot."

"Charlotte, you are a very strange friend indeed. I had hoped to present myself as a lady while in London, and I am quite certain, marksmanship is not on the list of accomplishments for a lady," said Elizabeth, her cheeks burning.

"Our Lizzy was a spirited young girl to be sure," said Mrs. Gardiner with a smile for Darcy as he walked into the room. "But, she has grown into a fine young lady. Anyone who has had the privilege of your company would agree."

"Thank you, Aunt," said Elizabeth giving Charlotte a hard stare.

"I have had some good news from Hertfordshire today," said Mr. Gardiner in an attempt to turn the subject. "Your father writes to inform us that Mary has accepted Mr. Collins' offer of marriage."

"It appears it is safe for you to return home, Miss Elizabeth," said Richard with a grin.

"So, it would seem, Colonel," said Elizabeth with good humour. Noting the look of confusion on Lord Matlock's face, Elizabeth said, "I am sure that this will do nothing to aid me in my quest to present myself as a proper young lady, but I shall spare you the confusion and explain. Mr. Collins is our cousin and due to an entail, my father's heir. He made an offer of marriage to me, which I, for very good reasons, refused. My mother was not pleased and for my good and my father's peace of mind, I was sent to London for a while. I am happy for Mary. She is much better suited to be a parson's wife."

"Your cousin is a parson? Does he have a parish?"

"He has the living at Hunsford," replied Elizabeth.

"He is my sister's parson?" asked Lord Matlock in surprise. "And pray how does he get along with Lady Catherine?"

Elizabeth chose her words carefully. "He speaks very highly of her. He has often told us about her, and he has described Rosings to us in such detail, I feel as though I have been there."

Lord Matlock laughed. "And does he speak of her advice—which she freely gives whether asked for or not on every subject?"

"I was told it was on her advice he came to choose a bride from among his cousins," said Elizabeth. "Although I am the only one to have refused Mr. Collins, there are two other ladies in this room—one who is related to me and one who is not—who were fortunate to avoid the same situation due to the interference of their mothers."

"Indeed?"

"Indeed. It seems it is now safe for Charlotte to return to Meryton which is quite opportune as her father, Sir William, is coming to escort her home in two days' time," said Elizabeth.

"We shall have to give her a proper sending off," said Bingley. "What say you, Darcy? Shall we gather at your house or mine?"

"I should think Darcy House would suit better. Is not your sister only arriving from Scarborough on the morrow? To ask her to host such a soiree on such short notice and after a long journey does not seem to be wise," replied Darcy. "Mrs. Davis will have no trouble arranging the details within two days' time. The children are welcome to attend, Mr. Gardiner. And, I will assume you will be joined by your sister, Bingley?"

"I will ask her. Would you and Richard like to stop by tomorrow evening? I could give you her answer then."

"Capital idea, my friend," said Richard.

"Now, Gardiner," said Lord Matlock. "There is the matter of that port you promised me."

Mr. Gardiner smiled and rose to leave.

"Darcy, I assume your invitation will reach your aunt tomorrow?"

"If not tonight, Uncle," replied Darcy.

"It has been a pleasure to meet you, ladies," said Lord Matlock with a bow. "I look forward to seeing you all again in two days' time. Miss Elizabeth, again, my best wishes for your health and recovery."

~*~*~*~*~*~

Mr. Gardiner poured a drink for himself and another for Lord Matlock.

"Your niece is a singular young lady." Lord Matlock settled into a chair in front of Mr. Gardiner's desk. "She is witty, well-spoken, and self-assured." He began enumerating Elizabeth's qualities—qualities he considered essential for the wife of his nephew. "She has a fondness for reading and the development of her mind. She cares deeply and is willing to risk her life to protect those she loves. She is obviously not a fortune hunter as she has refused the heir to her father's estate. She is not afraid to admit to her faults." He took the glass Mr.

Gardiner offered him. "I have to say I am impressed by her. And the attachment between her and my nephew seems to be equal. There is not much left for me to discuss with you. I assume that is why you insisted on my meeting her first?"

"Of course. I thought it best for Lizzy to speak for herself. But you still have questions, so please ask."

"What of her family? I know that her father is a landed gentleman, but what of his estate?"

"His estate is modest but well-run. He is a gracious landlord to his tenants, and they are quite loyal to him. It is publically known that his estate yields two thousand per annum, but those are only public numbers. His profits exceed this substantially. He keeps the profitability and even the organization of his estate somewhat a secret. He likes to keep people guessing—loves a good laugh, he does.

"However, the real reason that he keeps his finances secret is my sister, his wife. Fanny has always been a bit of a flibbertigibbet, but it has gotten worse as she has grown older. I believe it is because the estate is entailed away from her and her daughters. She is fearful of what will happen when Bennet passes." Mr. Gardiner sat his glass on the desk and leaned back in his chair. "I can assure you that her care has been provided for between myself and her husband. She shall have no need of want as long as she can live on an income of no more than two thousand a year. She can be a bit of a spendthrift, and to protect her from learning to live with more and having her circumstances lessen on his passing, Bennet has chosen to keep the true profitability of his estate a secret from her."

"I admire his forethought and desire to protect her," commented Lord Matlock.

"He does have an incredibly quick mind and a strong protective side. Elizabeth takes after her father in that regard. His protection extends to his daughters. The money for their dowries, which was merely one thousand a piece, is well-invested and has been gaining in value each year. Only he and I know the true numbers."

"But would not publishing their dowries make them available to a wider society in which to find a husband?"

"Indeed, it would, and perhaps with the younger girls, who are quite silly, publishing the amount may be necessary. However, Bennet knows the value of his eldest daughters and believed that they would be able to attract an appropriate husband without this number being known. He planned to share the true value of their dowry with them if the eldest remained unmarried at the age of three and twenty. Jane will be three and twenty in six month's time. However, I believe that the amount will be known sooner than that, now that Mary is engaged, and your nephew has requested of me permission to seek a courtship with Elizabeth."

"Darcy has talked to you?"

"Indeed he has, this morning at my warehouse. He plans to speak to you about it tonight. He will approach her father after Elizabeth and Jane have returned to Hertfordshire, but as he knows Lizzy is her father's favourite, he wishes a letter from me regarding the permission I have granted him here would precede him into Hertfordshire."

Lord Matlock guffawed. "He always was one who took every precaution to ensure success. I dare say, I never imagined he would ever have to worry about being refused. The fathers of the ton seem quite willing to throw their daughters in his direction."

"Bennet is not your typical father, and Elizabeth is not your typical lady." Mr. Gardiner leaned forward and rested his elbows on his desk, steepling his fingers in front of him and tapping the first two together as he considered his next question. Something Darcy had said during their interview that morning had him a bit uneasy for his niece's sake. He stopped tapping his fingers and folded them. "Do you fear she will not be accepted by your relations? Darcy mentioned something in that regard."

"My relations are traditionalists." Lord Matlock took a swallow of his drink. "They find my behaviour to be singular at times and not to their satisfaction. However, since I am the head of the family, they have no choice but to accept it. Although I cannot guarantee there will be no dissension, I think, for the most part, they will accept my position on Darcy's choice until they have met and are charmed by Miss Elizabeth." Lord Matlock grimaced slightly. "The only hold out will be my sister, Catherine. She has been under the impression Darcy would marry her daughter Anne since both Anne and Darcy were infants. I expect a loud confrontation and possibly a breach in the family fabric for a while, but it is not unexpected."

Mr. Gardiner's eyebrows rose. "Do I take it you approve of the possible match?"

"Without reservation," Lord Matlock replied flatly. "I have not seen Darcy as I did today since before his mother died, which was the last time he felt secure and unconditionally loved. I think he has found that feeling again, and I am glad for it. I look forward to the day when I can welcome you to my extended family, Gardiner."

Mr. Gardiner shook his head in disbelief. "Your family will then have ties to trade. Will that not be a sour taste for some?"

Lord Matlock placed his glass on the desk and leaned back in his chair with an amused smile on his face. "Gardiner, you are no ordinary tradesman. You are a well-respected businessman and member of the Mercer's Company." He tilted his head slightly and raised a quizzical brow, pausing until Mr. Gardiner nodded his acceptance of the facts. "That will do much to sweeten the taste; however, I will not lie and say it will not cause some trouble. But, it cannot be avoided. As you know from doing business with Darcy, he is a very determined man once he has made up his mind, and it appears he has made up his mind."

"Indeed it does. I wish him success."

"Well, then, Gardiner, I should head home. I look forward to seeing you at Darcy's."

~*~*~*~*~*~

"You know Father was here to check up on you, do you not?" said Richard when the gentlemen had entered the carriage.

"Yes, it was obvious to me, and I expect to Elizabeth as well," said Darcy.

"So it is Elizabeth now is it? Would Andrew still say you are a good gentleman if you use such familiar terms for Miss Elizabeth?" taunted Richard.

"Andrew knows it is acceptable for a gentleman to use a lady's Christian name during a courtship if the lady has given him permission."

"Courtship? Richard, did Darcy just say he was courting Miss Elizabeth?" asked Bingley.

"I believe he did, Bingley," replied Richard.

"Does this smack of impulsivity to you?"

"It does indeed. Seems more your style than his. What do you suppose has happened to him?"

"Perhaps you should ask him," said Darcy.

"Capital idea, Darcy. Do you think we should ask him, Richard?"

"I believe we must, Bingley."

"He may not answer you," said Darcy. "But if he did, he would probably say he had found a woman he could love and after seeing her bleeding in his arms, he had no wish to move any slower."

"Well, now, Bingley, see what he has gone and done? He has given such a reasonable answer we are left without means to tease him."

"Rather thoughtless of him, do you not think?" said Bingley with a smile. "So, when will this be official so I may inform my sister of her disappointment?"

Richard laughed.

"I have spoken to Elizabeth's uncle this morning, Elizabeth this afternoon and will speak to Uncle Matlock tonight and Elizabeth's father upon arriving in Hertfordshire. Mr. Gardiner is sending a letter regarding the permission he has granted me while Elizabeth is in London. It will not become a public courtship until I have spoken to her father, so you will just have to wait to share that news with your sister, Bingley. However, there is a disappointment of sorts that you shall wish to explain to her before both she and the Gardiners show up at my house."

Bingley smiled. "You mean the connection between my father and Miss Elizabeth's uncle?" The door to the carriage opened. "Why do you think I wanted you to come over tomorrow?" He chuckled as he stepped down from the carriage in front of his house.

"Just tell her before we get here," said Darcy.

Chapter 7

"Charles." Caroline strode purposefully into her brother's study. "Are there engagements of which I should take note? The holiday season in town can be quite busy." Taking a seat, she opened her calendar and took a pen from his desk. She had missed London society.

Charles pushed a few papers to the side and rummaged under a few more before finding his calendar. "We have a dinner at Darcy House tomorrow evening."

Caroline's smile was self-satisfied. How fortunate to be asked to dine with Mr. Darcy so soon after arriving in town. Perhaps he had missed her company while she was away?

"There will be several in attendance. Some of them you know and some you do not." Her brother both dreaded and relished the opportunity to share the information about the guests who would be present. "You, of course, know Colonel Fitzwilliam. He will be joined by his mother and father, Lord and Lady Matlock." Charles noted how her look of self-satisfaction grew to one of self-importance. "Our father's former partner, Mr. Edward Gardiner and his family will also be attending." She looked up from writing. "You have not had the privilege of meeting them, have you?"

She shook her head. "I know you do business with him quite regularly, but I have yet to have the pleasure of meeting him or his family."

"Mr. Gardiner is a highly respected business-man. Both Darcy and Lord Matlock are customers of long standing and count him a friend," said Charles with a sidelong glance at his sister. "Two of Gardiner's nieces will be joining them as well as some friends from Hertfordshire."

"From Hertfordshire?" said Caroline in surprise. "Who does Mr. Gardiner know in Hertfordshire?"

"He knows many people there, Caroline. He has family there." He paused for a moment allowing the shock of the news to settle in for a moment before he added to it. "Mrs. Bennet is his sister."

Caroline blanched at this knowledge. "Wh- Who are the nieces that are visiting the Gar- diners?"

"Miss Bennet and her sister Miss Elizabeth." Charles nearly laughed at the look of horror which passed quickly over his sister's face. "They have been joined these last two weeks by Miss Lucas and her sister Miss Maria, and Sir William is coming to collect his daughters. The dinner is in their hon- our. A going away soiree, so to speak."

Caroline was stunned. "And the Bennets? Do they return to Hertfordshire with Sir William?"

"No, they shall remain in town for another week. Then the Gardiners will go with them to cel- ebrate the season with family." He picked up some papers and moved them to a new pile on the desk as he braced himself for his sister's reply to the next bit of news. "I have asked Darcy and Georgiana to celebrate Christmas with us at Netherfield."

"Netherfield? We cannot spend the holidays at Netherfield." Rising to her feet, she slapped her calendar down on his desk. "You were not going to return until spring." She crossed her arms and glared at him. "Mr. Darcy has family in town or at

Pemberley. He cannot possibly wish to spend his Christmas in Hertfordshire!"

"Darcy has concluded the business keeping him in town. To travel to Pemberley at this time of year can be tricky." Charles leaned back in his chair. "Darcy insists it is important to spend at least part of the winter at Netherfield to determine the soundness of the house and agrees that it is only proper he visit so he can offer his opinion. However, if you prefer to stay in town with Louisa, I will understand and will not be offended. I know you find the society here more agreeable than in the country." Charles quietly hoped that Caroline would decide to remain in London. "I do not think you should decide in haste, Caroline. I do not plan to travel to Netherfield for a fortnight. You can give me your decision next week.

"We will, of course, be hosting a dinner for the Gardiners and their relations while they are in Hertfordshire. It is only proper. Without Gardiner buying out Father's share of the business, I would not have been able to consider owning an estate, and you would not be able to move in the society in which you do. And your dowry would not be what it is."

Caroline gasped. Her eyes widened in understanding and revulsion. Relations of the Bennets were the source of her good fortune? It was almost more than she could countenance. In her haste to exit the room, she nearly collided with Mr. Jennings, who was on his way to announce the arrival of Mr. Darcy and Colonel Fitzwilliam. Caroline mumbled a greeting to the gentlemen and hurried on her way.

"I see she took the news well?" quipped Richard.

"Well enough for the present, but I am sure I will hear more about it later once she finds her tongue." He motioned for them to take a seat. "I do not remember the last time she was speechless."

"Nor has she ever said so few words in greeting to Darcy," said Richard with a laugh.

"Perhaps I told her too many disappointing pieces of information at once," said Bingley.

"Exactly what did you tell her?" Darcy eyed his friend suspiciously.

"I did not tell her that," said Bingley. "I merely acquainted her with the idea that Father's business partner is related to the Bennets, and that I would be returning to Netherfield with you and Georgiana for the holidays rather than staying in town. I have given her until next week to decide if she will travel with me or remain here. Of course, I would rather that she stays in town, but I have left the decision up to her."

"And will she be attending dinner tomorrow evening?" Darcy took the glass of brandy Bingley offered.

"I did not ask her. I just told her we were attending. I think she needs to see certain people in company to prepare herself for future disappointments," said Bingley with a grin. "And are your aunt and uncle attending?"

"Yes, they will be there tomorrow night. My aunt is especially interested in meeting everyone. Uncle Matlock has told her about the various people he met yesterday, and his account seems to have her intrigued."

"I believe it was the account of a particular young lady that has piqued her interest," said Richard.

Caroline, who had come to retrieve her calendar, paused outside the study. She felt faint. Lord Matlock had already met the others who would be attending the dinner? And his wife wanted to meet one young lady in particular? Were they talking about—no, it could not be. Certainly Darcy had not fallen for that chit Elizabeth Bennet, had he? This would not do. No, this would not do at all. Leaving her calendar until later, Caroline stalked off to her room to plan tomorrow evening's attack. The first order of business was making sure that her best dress was ready.

~*~*~*~*~

Elizabeth sighed in frustration as she attempted to smooth her gown and check her hair. Jane gave her a knowing smile and finished the tasks for her.

"Do not fret, Lizzy. You look beautiful," she whispered.

"Thank you," Elizabeth whispered back. "But, I shall never be as beautiful as you."

"I think you outshine me in at least one person's eyes," Jane teased as the carriage door opened, and they saw Mr. Darcy waiting to assist them.

Elizabeth's cheeks flushed.

"So good to see you, sir," bubbled the effervescent Sir William. "It is such an honour to be asked to dine with you tonight." He exited the carriage and handed his daughters out. Then, with a wink at Elizabeth, he stepped away to allow Mr. Darcy to assist first Jane and then Elizabeth.

Darcy took Elizabeth's hand and carefully guided her out of the carriage, keeping a watchful eye on her injured arm. Then, instead of releasing her hand, he placed it firmly in the crook of his arm. "We must not risk further injury," he said in a low voice.

"Quite right, sir. Having only one arm can throw off one's balance." He placed his free hand over hers and led her into the house. Elizabeth took in the grandeur of the house. The ceilings were high, and the furnishings were elegant but not overly so. She caught Darcy watching her.

"Do you like it?" There was a hint of nervousness in his voice.

"Very much."

"I am glad." He helped her with her wrap and then stepped away so that his sister might greet her.

Several footmen scurried out the door as two more carriages arrived. The first carried the rest of the Gardiner party while the second belonged to Lord Matlock. Soon the grand entry hall was filled with laughter and talking as introductions were made, and outerwear was removed. Just as the group was moving into the drawing room, Mr. Bingley's carriage arrived, and introductions were made a second time.

"I see the doctor has allowed you to start walking, Master Andrew," said Bingley.

"Oh, yes, I can walk on my leg a bit, but I mustn't put my full weight on it for a few more days. That is why I have this crutch," explained Andrew in a most serious tone. "My Lizzy is also able to walk around now, but she mustn't use her arm yet. Bone takes longer to heal than skin—that is what the doctor said."

"I am very glad to hear that you are listening so closely to the doctor's instructions," said Bingley. "I see your sisters and brother are heading upstairs to play, do you require assistance?"

"Yes, sir. I am not very good at using my crutch on the stairs. I just started using it today, and it is going to take some practice," said Andrew.

"May I carry you up the stairs?" asked Bingley.

Andrew smiled. "I would like that."

~*~*~*~*~*~

"They are set up for a right proper good time up there. I was tempted to stay and play with the soldiers." Bingley took a chair next to Jane in the drawing room.

Conversation had flowed freely about the room for some time before Caroline decided to attempt her first try at disparaging Elizabeth. She had noticed Elizabeth's injured arm and was certain it was the result of some unladylike behaviour.

"Miss Eliza, whatever have you done to your arm?"

"Oh, I have done nothing to it, but the doctor has stitched it up and confined it to this sling. Of course, he has only done that because someone else decided to shoot me," said Elizabeth playfully.

"Shoot you?" cried Caroline, her hand flying up to her heart in astonishment.

"Yes, Miss Bingley. But, I assure you I was not his actual target at the time. My cousin Andrew was."

"And Miss Elizabeth was shot while protecting Master Andrew and disarming the villain." Bingley, fully aware of what his sister was attempting, glared at her. "It happened just three days ago."

"Oh, how fortunate," Caroline muttered.

"Indeed it was," said her brother.

"I quite agree," said Darcy. "Now, Mrs. Gardiner, would you and your nieces like a tour of Darcy House?"

"Thank you, Mr. Darcy. I should like that very much, and it would give me an excuse to check on the children before we dine."

So it was decided, and the tour began with a stop on the upper floor at the nursery.

After a few moments in the nursery and satisfied that her children were behaving, Mrs. Gardiner was ready to begin the tour in earnest. However, they were delayed by the insistence of the children –Andrew, in particular, –that Elizabeth see the game that he and Michael were playing. Patiently, she stooped to look at the fort they had built and commented on the fine arrangement of toy soldiers that were encamped among the pillows and blocks. Then, with a quick kiss for each, she hurried to join the other adults who were waiting at the door.

Lady Matlock smiled and ticked off the quality of capable and caring mother in her mind. Her husband had come home extolling the virtues of a country miss that had captured their nephew's heart. As much as she believed his report, she needed to see the girl herself to assess her appropriateness for the nephew who was as much a son to her as her own boys. She had already noted the humor and humility Elizabeth had displayed when responding to Miss Bingley regarding the injury to her arm. She had given only the facts and had blushed when Mr. Bingley had mentioned her rather heroic actions.

Lady Matlock continued to watch the reactions of Elizabeth to the fine features of Darcy House. She looked for any indication of fortune hunting, but none appeared in Miss Elizabeth—Miss Bingley, on the other hand, caused Lady Matlock to shake her head in dismay on more than one occasion. Miss Bingley hinted at the expense of several items while Elizabeth commented only on their aesthetics or asked genuine questions of interest about them. Genuine, Lady Matlock checked off another quality in her mind.

They had reached the library on the first floor by this time, and Lady Matlock could almost feel the excitement that exuded from Elizabeth before the door to the library had even opened. A lover of books, she checked off. Darcy was an intellectual and a marriage to a woman without the love of reading and improving her mind would only bring him misery. The door to the library opened almost as wide as Elizabeth's eyes at the sight of the rows of books lining the walls from floor to ceiling. She gasped, and her hand flew up to her mouth. Slowly, reverently, she stepped into the room and began to walk the perimeter, noting the titles on the books, running her fingers along their spines, and occasionally stopping to pull one out just enough to look at its cover.

Darcy watched her from the other side of the room while he talked with Mr. Gardiner about the collection. Without thinking, he busied his hands straightening a chair here or a book on a table there. Elizabeth noted his actions and leaned toward Georgiana and asked, "Is he always so fastidious?"

Georgiana laughed. "Yes, Fitzwilliam does like order a bit too much at times." Lady Matlock agreed with this statement wholeheartedly; Darcy was on the obsessive side of order.

Elizabeth's eyes sparkled with mischief. "Perhaps we should give him something to do?" she asked conspiratorially. She pushed the book she had been looking at on the shelf back into place, stopping short of pushing it flush with the others.

She moved down a shelf and pulled out three more books, just far enough to make them appear out of place.

"There, enough to give him something to do, but not enough to put him in a foul humour," she said to Georgiana, who giggled. "Shall we watch to see how long it takes him to fix it?"

She and Georgiana took seats in two over-stuffed leather chairs and watched as Darcy and Mr. Gardiner drew near to the sabotaged shelves. They both erupted into soft peals of laughter as Darcy still in conversation with Mr. Gardiner, straightened the books making sure the spines were just flush.

Lady Matlock watched the events as she moved to join Mrs. Gardiner, who was studying an atlas on a nearby table. A pleasant tease and a companion for Georgiana, Lady Matlock ticked off two more from her list of criteria. During dinner, she noticed the grace and good manners that Miss Elizabeth displayed as well as her ability to converse easily and draw everyone around her into conversation, including the normally reticent Darcy. Lady Matlock only had two major concerns left. One was regarding the ability of Miss Elizabeth to run a household as large as Pemberley, which could not be fully discerned in an evening; however, with Elizabeth's obviously keen mind, the skills could be learned. The second remaining concern was regarding how she would handle the disapprobation of certain members of the ton. Again, it was something that might not easily be determined in one evening–especially amongst friends.

Caroline had been out of sorts all evening. Elizabeth had occupied all of Darcy's attention, and his relatives seemed to be falling for her charms as well. Every attempt to discredit her had failed. Trying not to be utterly discouraged, Caroline decided to try one more time to disgrace Elizabeth in the eyes of Lord and Lady Matlock.

"I understand the militia remains in Meryton," she said coyly. "I imagine that is a delight to your family. I remember there were certain members who were favourites of your sisters."

Elizabeth's eyes flashed, but not with amusement. She clenched her jaw just slightly but forced herself to smile. "All of Meryton has enjoyed having the militia encamped there. It is quite an economic advantage to most merchants, and Sir William has arranged many events to provide entertainment, not only for those who serve His Majesty, but also our friends and neighbours. However, not all of the officers remain," she spoke in a friendly fashion with just a hint of coolness in her tone.

"Not all remain?" Caroline had a sense that this conversation, like all the others that evening, was not going to go in her favour.

"Yes, one, in particular," said Richard, who had just returned to the room after having been summoned to talk to a caller at the door. "That was one of my men; he called to inform me there is a frigate sailing out of Portsmouth within a week." He looked to Darcy with a slight menacing smile. "It seems there is a captain, with a reputation for being extremely exacting, in need of men before he sails toward the Americas, so Wickham will be on his way to join it in the morning. He may be engaged in battle before long."

"Mr. Wickham has joined the navy?" Caroline was confused.

"Not of his own accord, but it seems he preferred that option to hanging." Richard dared not look at his mother for he was sure to see her displeasure at his broaching such a topic with ladies present, but his patience with Miss Bingley had been stretched to its limit. "It was Wickham who shot Miss Elizabeth and her cousin."

Caroline gasped; this conversation was not going as she had planned. She knew she should let it drop, but curiosity got the better of her. "Why ever would he do that?"

"Misplaced vengeance," replied Elizabeth. "It seems he holds Mr. Darcy responsible for his situation in life, but he is too smart to attack the man himself. So, he attacks those who are his friends. I suppose he figured abduction of a child or a woman would play on Mr. Darcy's sensibilities most effectively, would you not agree?"

Unable to refute the question, Caroline allowed it to be so.

"And by playing on those sensibilities, Wickham purposed to acquire that which he desired." Elizabeth sat quietly and considered Caroline for a moment. "People like Wickham have always been a part of society, I suppose. You do not have to look far into a history book to find stories of nefarious individuals willing to destroy whatever or whomever they chose to get what they desire." She held Caroline's gaze. "Sadly, such actions are not just confined to the rich and powerful figures of history. These actions surround us every day on a smaller scale. It is, I believe, our Christian duty to rise above such scheming, for doing so is the only true way to improve society." Elizabeth looked Caroline levelly in the eyes.

Able to handle the ton. Lady Matlock checked off the last item on her list. She had witnessed the cattiness of women like Miss Bingley portrayed time and again within the ton, but never had she seen a more diplomatic and thorough set down. She smiled at Elizabeth and shared a knowing look with her husband. This was the only woman her nephew should marry.

"And that, my friends, is why she is one of the brightest jewels in the county—beautiful and clever. Quite a dangerous combination." Sir William stood and gave her a fatherly pat on the shoulder and a knowing wink. "I hate to put a stop to a fine time, but we are leaving quite early in the morning. Now, Charlotte, do you remember where the music room is? I believe your sister is there with Miss Darcy and the two Miss Gardiners."

Charlotte nodded. "I believe I do. Shall I fetch Amelia and Margaret for you, Mrs. Gardiner?"

"Thank you, my dear. That would be most helpful."

"I would be happy to be of assistance, Miss Lucas," Richard offered.

Charlotte smiled as she accepted his proffered arm. "I am quite sure I can find my way by following the music, sir, but your company would not be unwelcome. You are aware, we shall be bombarded with exclamations of delight from three young girls?"

Richard laughed as he led her from the room. "I believe I can sustain such an unpleasant attack for a few moments."

A flurry of activity followed their departure. Bingley called for his carriage while his sister sought her wrap, and the Gardiners made for the nursery to collect their children. Lord Matlock extended his wishes for a speedy and safe journey to Sir William, and Lady Matlock extended an invitation to Elizabeth, Jane and their aunt to join her and Georgiana for tea the following week.

Darcy was pleased with his aunt's invitation. He knew the approbation he had received from his uncle regarding his choice of Elizabeth was important, but he also knew the real approval needed to come from his aunt.

After wishing a good night and safe travels to Charlotte and Maria, Richard stood next to his cousin. "So, Mother approves?"

"Apparently," said Darcy. "Are you leaving or staying?"

"I think, I shall stay if you are up to billiards and brandy?" said Richard.

"As always," said Darcy with a grin, following him into the entry.

"Might I be of assistance, Mrs. Gardiner?" The Gardiners had returned from the nursery, and Mrs. Gardiner had a sleeping Michael snuggled in her arms. "I can hand him into the carriage for you."

"Thank you, Mr. Darcy." Mrs. Gardiner passed him the child. Michael stirred just enough to see who held him before contentedly wrapping his arms around Darcy's neck and laying his head on the gentleman's shoulder.

Elizabeth slipped her hand into Darcy's arm. "Can you manage both my cousin and me?"

"Certainly, Miss Elizabeth." He smiled back at her.

One by one, the various guests left Darcy

House and climbed aboard the waiting carriages. Having seen to his sister and then Jane, Bingley waited beside Sir William's carriage as Darcy first handed Michael into the Gardiner carriage before proceeding in his direction with Elizabeth on his arm.

"I wanted to thank you for hosting such a fine soiree," He said as Darcy approached. "I would stay and play billiards, but I have a rather disappointed sister to take home and contend with. Miss Elizabeth, thank you for so elegantly dealing with Caroline this evening. I apologize for her behaviour..."

She held up a hand to stop him. "I cannot hold you responsible for anyone's actions save your own, Mr. Bingley. I, of all people, know full well that a sister may act without regard for others in her family."

"Your understanding is appreciated." He gave her a small bow and headed to his carriage and his sister.

Darcy and Elizabeth stood toward the front of Sir William's carriage. The light from the carriage's lanterns danced and flickered, playing with the shadows. Darcy took a step closer to Elizabeth and took her hand.

"I want you to think about something, for me. Do not answer me right away and know that I will be pleased with either answer."

"That sounds ominous, Fitzwilliam."

"It is nothing dire, my dear. I just wish to know how to proceed when I get to Hertfordshire. Do you wish for me to request a public courtship, or would you prefer that I ask for an engagement? No," he said laying a finger on her lips to stop her from speaking, "I do not want you to answer me tonight. Remember, I will be happy either way. I love you and intend to spend my whole life demonstrating to you just how much, so either way, as long as you are in my life, I will always be happy. Frustrated because I wish to kiss you and hold you, but happy."

"I will think about it Fitzwilliam." Elizabeth looked about and being assured no one was watching, she rose up on her toes and kissed him on the cheek. "You may have promised Andrew not to kiss me until we are standing under a gauge at the end of a court, but I made no such promise."

"He would say you were not being a good lady, Elizabeth," warned Darcy.

"I am sure you are correct, sir," she said as she

kissed him again. "Good night, my love," she whispered.

"You are making it very hard for me to be a good gentleman," growled Darcy.

"So, you would still be happy with either answer?" she teased and moved toward the carriage and into the line of sight of the occupants.

"I will not lie. One answer would make me happier than the other, but my goal is not just my happiness but yours, Elizabeth." He pulled her back and gave her hand a kiss before handing her into the carriage.

~*~*~*~*~*~

Richard chuckled and dropped the curtain back into place. He was happy for his cousin, but there was a strange gnawing in his stomach, a restlessness that had not been there before. It felt as if something or someone was missing. As he pulled back the curtain one more time and watched the Lucas's carriage roll away, he knew who. She was not even around the corner, and he missed her already? He shook his head at the addled state of his brain. Tomorrow, he would be returning to the routine of his regiment for two weeks. That should help him focus.

"Are you prepared to be soundly beaten?" asked Darcy good-naturedly as he strolled into the billiards room.

"Do your worst, cousin," said Richard with a grin. "I return to my regiment for a fortnight beginning tomorrow. Do you think Bingley would let me join you and Georgie?"

"I cannot imagine he would say no." Darcy circled the table studying his shot.

"I am selling out, Darcy. I am tired of the life, and I have the small estate that Father has kept for me. According to my calculations, with the income from the estate, the funds I have set aside, and the money from selling my commission, I will be solvent. I have only been living on half pay for a year now and banking the rest. But, I have very little experience running an estate. I thought perhaps I could come listen to you lecture Bingley and with any luck, learn a few things."

"You are selling out?" Darcy stood with his cue resting on the table, his shot clearly forgotten in the light of Richard's news. "I knew you would eventually; I just did not expect it so soon. Of course, I will gladly share any advice with you that you need, and probably some you will not."

Richard laughed, "Of that I have no doubt, cousin."

"Are you still thinking of raising horses?"

"I am good with horses."

"I know." Darcy took a seat near his cousin and accepted the drink that had been poured for him. "I think it is wise to stick with what you know. It is easier to do the work when you enjoy it. But, it will be a big change. Estate management can be tedious. Are you prepared for that?"

"Darcy, I have been running most of the accounts on my unit by myself for the last six months. I assure you, I do not need to be told how tedious it is. I needed to see if I could do it, and I can. I cannot say I enjoy it, but I can do it."

"So, you have thought this through quite carefully. Have you spoken to your father yet?"

"No, I plan to speak to him during the holidays, but I do not expect any trouble from that front. Mother has been asking when I was going to settle down, and if I have her support..."

"Your father's will follow," Darcy finished Richard's thought. "When she talked about you settling down, was she implying just selling out or did it include marriage?"

"Oh, you know Mother. She is looking for the grandmother experience, but I should have some time on my side there—thanks to you," Richard said with a grin. "I have been keeping my eyes open for a while now. Not much quality in the marriage mart these days. Perhaps I will have to go out of town like you and Bingley."

"There is always Charlotte Lucas," said Darcy watching Richard's face closely. Richard's eyes flinched a minuscule amount, and Darcy smiled to himself. "She is not an heiress, but according to Elizabeth, all she wants is a secure position some-where, it does not have to be grand. Elizabeth said that was why Charlotte's mother sent her to the Gardiners. She was afraid Charlotte would settle for Mr. Collins just to gain a secure position where she would not be a burden to her family."

"I do not want someone who will settle for me," Richard said with a huff.

"I did not say she would be settling for you. I said she would have settled for Collins. So, if that twitch in your eye is any indication of what you truly think about her, you might wish to move quickly. If she would settle for Collins, she will not be the one sent away because she refused an offer of marriage."

"Darcy, Father and Mother might be willing to accept a country miss for you, but I am not sure they would for me. They have expectations that I should marry well, which means marrying someone with money."

"Richard, listen carefully. If you find that you love her, I will help you convince your parents she is the right choice," said Darcy. "Do not settle for money alone. You and I have both seen the misery that usually follows in the wake of marriages arranged solely on the advantage of wealth or position."

"Thank you, Darcy. I know I tease you about being so blasted steady and responsible, but that is what makes you such a good friend." He drained his glass and stood. "Now, enough of the sappy talk, let's play.

Chapter 8

The sun had just made its way above the horizon when the Lucas carriage left Gracechurch Street. The air was crisp, but the brilliance of the morning light promised a pleasant day. Knowing how much her nieces enjoyed a good walk, Mrs. Gardiner suggested that Jane and Elizabeth, as well as her daughters, accompany her on her morning calls, one of which was a delivery of cloth to a charity, a hospital for fallen girls, near Hyde Park.

Not far from the park at Darcy House, Richard was preparing to rejoin his unit when an officer arrived with an urgent message.

"Escaped!" Richard roared.

Lieutenant Artman shrank back. "Yes, sir, I was told he broke away from the detail escorting him to the dock, sir. We believe he had help, sir. "

"You were not there?"

"No, sir. Dawes has the detail confined until the scheme has been deciphered."

Richard paced the entrance, circling the young lieutenant. "He was headed in this general direction, you say?"

"We thought he might be coming here, sir."

"Who might be here?" asked Darcy coming down the stairs in his riding clothes.

Richard stepped in front of Lieutenant Artman. "Wickham."

Darcy slowly and deliberately took the last few steps to the bottom of the staircase. "Impossible. He is sailing to Portsmouth this morning to take up his new position under Captain Buchannan." His voice was low and steady, a sign he was trying to contain his true emotions.

"That was the plan, but things have changed. He has made an escape."

Darcy staggered backwards as if he had been dealt a blow. His eyes grew wide as a frightening thought crossed his mind. "He is not coming here. He first saw Elizabeth at the park and knows her love of walking."

"That may be, but Miss Elizabeth is in

Gracechurch Street. Hyde Park is a significant drive even at this early hour."

Darcy shook his head. "Mrs. Gardiner is delivering cloth to the hospital..."

"Near Hyde Park," Richard concluded. "You are going riding there this morning?"

"I am."

"You have a horse, Artman?"

"Yes, sir."

"Bring it around to the mews. Darcy and I will meet you there."

"Sir?" Lieutenant Artman looked at Darcy and then back to Richard with a question in his eye.

"He will not stay here even if we ask him to." Richard stepped closer to the officer and lowered his voice. "My displeasure is nothing compared to his. Do not let his calm exterior fool you. Beneath it lies a raging lion. I will make sure he knows to follow my lead."

Lieutenant Artman nodded. "I will get my horse, sir."

~*~*~*~*~*~

Jane, Elizabeth, and their cousins had just rounded a corner in a less frequented area of the park and were on their way to meet their aunt at

155

the carriage, when a man who had been leaning against a tree stepped onto the path next to Elizabeth.

"Miss Elizabeth, it is a pleasure to see you this morning."

"I heard you were planning a voyage, Mr. Wickham." Elizabeth tried to move away from him, but he grabbed her injured arm pulling it out of its sling while dragging her back firmly against him.

"Yes, it seems his majesty's navy has need of me, but when I saw you entering the park earlier, I knew I could not leave without a proper goodbye." He wrenched her arm behind her back causing her to cry out in pain. "My apologies. Did that hurt?" He twisted her arm a bit harder.

"Not as much as you will when I have finished with you," spat Elizabeth.

"You, hurt me? A pretty little thing like you? 'Tis a pity there are no books around for you to use as weapons." He laughed.

Elizabeth's eyes flashed, and she looked at Jane. "Jane, dearest," she said in a frighteningly calm and cool voice, "Mr. Wickham thinks I need weapons."

"How silly of him," said Jane. "Margaret, take Amelia and tell Aunt we will be along shortly. Lizzy and I would like to play a game of Master Marsden. Be quick, we would not want her to worry." The young girls hesitated a moment. "All will be well," Jane whispered. "Your mother will understand my meaning." She gave them a small push to start them moving.

A few yards away, the confrontation was being watched closely. Lieutenant Artman had noticed Wickham standing near a tree and the three had crept up on him, hoping to prevent his dashing away. They had nearly reached their goal when the ladies had come around the corner and Wickham had taken hold of Elizabeth.

Richard placed a hand on his cousin's chest to stay him. He crouched behind a bush, pulling a reluctant Darcy with him. "He does not know we are here. We can spring on him at any moment if needed, but he is holding her arm at such an awkward angle. I do not wish to chance further injury. Nor do we know if he is armed." He grabbed his cousin by the shoulders forcing Darcy to look at him. "I will not let him hurt her. Do you trust me?"

Darcy nodded his assent. He did not like to helplessly watch, but he trusted Richard's instincts.

Richard gave a flick of his hand toward the opposite side of the path and Artman moved to a position behind another bush. "If I signal to Artman to move, you are to remain here until Wickham is under our power. If he sees you, it will only make matters more dangerous for Miss Elizabeth."

Again Darcy nodded his head.

Jane caught the motion of Artman as he took his position. The sight of his uniform brought a bit of calm to her heart. She glanced to where he had come from and noted another uniform and the blue of a gentleman's coat. She smiled and walked closer to Elizabeth. She was certain her sister could handle this situation, but the knowledge that help was so near bolstered her confidence. "Would you like me to hold your reticule, Elizabeth?"

"Your assistance would be appreciated." Elizabeth handed her reticule to Jane.

"Do you require any further help?" Jane stood calmly before her sister.

"What game did you tell Margaret we were playing?"

"Master Marsden."

"Like we played with Billy back in Meryton?"

"Yes, at the assembly."

"What are you yammering about?" asked Wickham in exasperation.

"Why, Mr. Wickham," began Jane in a condescending tone. "I have always been something of a second for my sister when she got herself into a skirmish. I was merely performing my duties—making sure she is ready and truly wishes to go through with this. Surely you know what a second is?" Jane moved away slightly.

"Of course I know what a second is," sputtered Wickham. "But you are females."

"How good of you to notice," muttered Elizabeth as she looked to Jane. Jane gave her a small nod. A quick flurry of activity followed, and Wickham lay on his side moaning, his knees drawn up towards his waist, his hands clutching his abdomen, blood flowing from his nose. Elizabeth knelt on him, grinding her knee into his side. "Jane, your ribbon?"

Jane pulled the ribbon from around the waist of her dress and used it to securely bind Wickham's hands.

"Wait here until he is in Artman's grasp and well away from Miss Elizabeth," whispered Richard. Seeing his cousin was reluctant to comply, he added, "We must ensure her safety." A small growling sound signalled Darcy's acquiescence.

"Mind if Artman here relieves you of this blackguard?" Richard asked stepping from his hiding place.

"Colonel!" exclaimed Elizabeth accepting his assistance in getting to her feet. "You may gladly do whatever you wish with the scoundrel." She smoothed her skirt and straightened her jacket.

Artman hauled Wickham to his feet none too gently and moved him away from the ladies.

"That was impressive, Miss Elizabeth," said Richard. He motioned for Darcy to join them.

"Charlotte did tell you her aim was legendary, did she not?" asked Jane sweetly.

"Yes, but I thought she was talking about throwing things like books and rocks, not elbows and punches," said Richard.

"Well, that is part of it. You should also be aware that her aim is quite good with a gun and a sword as well," said Jane. She laughed at the look of exasperation on Elizabeth's face.

"And were you often her second?" Darcy asked

Jane, a small teasing curve to his lips. He was much relieved to have Elizabeth at his side.

"Whenever Charlotte was not available." Elizabeth narrowed her eyes and raised a brow at her sister. "Do not let Jane's sweetness fool you. Her aim is nearly as good as mine, but her true talent lies in her proficiency with knots. How long did it take Master Marsden to get out of those knots, Jane?"

"I think he was still tied up in the cloakroom when his father came to get his mother's wrap," said Jane.

"Master Marsden—that is the game you told Miss Margaret you were going to play, is it not?" asked Darcy.

Jane nodded. "A code. Aunt knows about what happened with Mr. Marsden so she will be—oh, here she comes, now." Mrs. Gardiner was rushing down the path towards them followed closely by her footman, Jonathan, and her daughters. "I knew that message would rouse her to come quickly," continued Jane. "Although I am certain Elizabeth had already noted Mr. Wickham was unarmed, the code assured her of the accuracy of her assessment."

"And if he had been armed?" asked Richard in fascination.

"Well, then we would have been playing Jacob Lucas or Jeremy Woods, I suppose," said Jane. "Depending on the type of weapon, of course."

Richard shook his head in disbelief. "I do not have soldiers who are as adept as you two at disarming enemies."

"Well, when you are a girl and the champion of all sorts of boy's games, you become a target of many who wish to claim back the title for their gender." Elizabeth held her injured arm firmly against her side, her hand resting on her abdomen.

"And when boys like Billy Madison finally realize that girls are good for more than rock throwing competitions, and they become a little too friendly at assemblies, you get additional practice." Jane laughed. "Perhaps that is why you have such a hard time getting a man to stand up with you at assemblies, Lizzy. I do not think one of them has come away from childhood without their egos and many of their persons scarred by you."

Darcy and Richard laughed. "Did you ever have to step in as the second?" asked Darcy.

"Not once," said Jane. "And Charlotte and I

always won our skirmishes without much resistance once the boys knew Lizzy was our second."

"You make me sound horrid." Elizabeth began to unbutton her pelisse. "I assure you I was not a ruffian. I just could not tolerate someone—especially a boy—beating me at, well, just about anything."

"Oh, Lizzy, Jane, I am so relieved to see you standing and in one piece." Mrs. Gardiner gasped slightly for breath. She had very nearly run the entire way from the carriage to the park when Margaret had relayed Jane's message. She threw her arms around first Jane and then Elizabeth. "When Maggie told me what you were playing...I feared I might be too late." She turned to the gentlemen. "Will you be joining us at Gracechurch for tea?"

"My apologies, Mrs. Gardiner, but I will not be able to accept your kind offer," said Richard. "I wish to personally ensure this miscreant boards his ship. Then, I must return to my unit as required." He gave a bow and joined Lieutenant Artman.

"I would be happy to accept," said Darcy.

"I would like to see the doctor," said Elizabeth as she struggled with the last button of her jacket. All eyes turned to her in concern. Finally, with a bit of assistance from Jane, she shrugged her arm out of her coat revealing a blood-stained sleeve.. "It seems my wound has reopened. I think the pulling and twisting caused the stitches to tear," she explained. "Aunt, do you have bandages in your kit?" Elizabeth pointed to the bag that her aunt was carrying. "If you do, could you please bind the wound?" She attempted to take a step towards her aunt but swayed unsteadily. She blinked her eyes to clear her vision. "I think I require a bench," she said as she began to feel her knees wobble.

Darcy swept Elizabeth into his arms, carried her to a nearby bench and placed her on it, sitting down next to her. "Jonathan," Darcy addressed the Gardiner's footman, "have Dr. Clarke and Mr. Thompson come to Darcy House. It is closer." He turned to Mrs. Garner. "I believe I shall host the tea today if you find that acceptable."

Mrs. Gardiner, who had just finished wrapping her niece's arm, nodded her approval. "I would feel better having Lizzy tended to before she has to ride for any distance in a carriage. It may not make her more comfortable, but it will make me more comfortable." She bit her lip and looked about. "I am not sure Lizzy will make the walk to the carriage under her own power."

"My horse is just back a bit. Allow me to fetch him, and then if you or Jane would help Elizabeth onto the horse, she can ride in front of me." Despite Elizabeth's protests of being well and the impropriety of such a suggestion, it was decided that Jane would assist Elizabeth onto the horse. Once Elizabeth had mounted the horse and was secured snuggly within Darcy's embrace, Jane and Mrs. Gardiner headed for their carriage.

"Are you well?" Darcy asked.

"To own the truth, I have been better," Elizabeth gave him a wry smile. "My arm is quite sore, and I am tired. Perhaps my strength is not quite up to fighting off villains. I cannot say that any of the neighbourhood boys ever truly posed a threat to anything more than my pride or my virtue. I think fearing for your mortal safety is quite all-consuming. I do not know how soldiers handle it. Colonel Fitzwilliam must be so tired." Elizabeth rested her head against Darcy's shoulder.

"He is," said Darcy as he urged his horse into a walk. "He told me last night that he is thinking of selling out and settling down."

"Mmm, that sounds like a good idea," said Elizabeth. "Will he be looking to take a wife?"

"I think he already is," said Darcy.

"Do you think you could put in a good word for Charlotte? She seems quite taken with him, and I really think they would do well together." Elizabeth tilted her head to look up at him.

"I do not need to put in a good word for Miss Lucas, my love. Richard seems quite taken with her as well. He is just not sure about his parents' reaction to the idea. He is under the impression that his family expects a more advantageous alliance," said Darcy. "But I have assured him that if he truly loves her, I will go to his father with him, and I will do what I can to assist. I want him to be as happy as I am with you."

"Charlotte is not without dowry or inheritance. Her father has been tucking away money for her on the sly just as mine has for my sisters and me. I am not supposed to know, but I was sitting outside the window to my father's study last summer and happened to overhear a conversation."

"Why would they keep that information a secret?" asked Darcy in bewilderment.

"Because they love their daughters and do not

wish for them to be sought after for monetary reasons," said Elizabeth. "Can you imagine being hunted for your money?" she added with a little laugh.

Darcy snorted. "Indeed I can. I guess it would be nice to not be so and so with such and such pounds per year. I have heard it all my adult life. That is Mr. Darcy of Pemberley. He has ten thousand a year." Darcy laughed. "Of course, like your father, I have kept my real value a secret as well. I am worth more than ten thousand a year."

"More than ten thousand?" Elizabeth said in amazement.

"Yes, my love," said Darcy giving her a squeeze.

"Do not worry. I shall not tell my mother. Ten thousand a year is enough to set her a flutter," said Elizabeth with a laugh. "You do know, Fitzwilliam, that I do not care how much you do or do not have. I love you for you, nothing else."

"I know, Elizabeth, and I love you with or without a cent to your name, and in spite of your mother's fluttering." He smiled down at her. She giggled.

"I have been thinking about what you asked me last night." She played with one of the buttons on his coat. "I think you should ask my father for permission to marry me."

"Are you sure? Do you really wish to marry me?" asked Darcy hopefully.

"Quite sure. I would be quite happy, Mr. Darcy, to be your wife."

"Does this mean we are standing under a gauge?" He asked with a grin, reining his horse to a stop.

"Why I believe it does, sir. Although we appear to be sitting. Only the horse is standing," replied Elizabeth looking up at him with an impertinent smile. Noting the look in his eyes, she added, "But, I must remind you, we are in public, and very good gentlemen do not kiss ladies in public."

"Perhaps I am not such a good gentleman after all," said Darcy as he tilted her chin and kissed her gently. "I love you, Elizabeth Bennet, and frankly I do not care who knows. Now, shall we get you home so the doctor can fix you up...again?"

Chapter 9

The next week was a busy one at the Gardiner's home. There were many preparations to be made for a family with four children before making the journey to Longbourn. The day before their departure for Hertfordshire, Georgiana came to call on Elizabeth while Jane and Mrs. Gardiner were out.

"Georgiana, do you think he will like it?" Elizabeth pulled in her lip and bit it as she held up the cravat she had just finished stitching.

"Elizabeth, it is a cravat," said Georgiana. "It looks just like the ones he wears. I am sure he will like it."

"And the book?" said Elizabeth apprehensively.

"It is one of his favourite authors." Georgiana put an arm around Elizabeth's shoulder. "I think you could wrap up a rock, and he would cherish it."

"I hardly think anyone could cherish a rock,"

stated Elizabeth. "I just want my presents to be useful and appreciated."

"They will be. Please stop worrying."

"I will try, but this is all so strange." Elizabeth coloured slightly. "The only men I have ever given gifts to are my father and uncles, and well, this is different." She hurried on trying to explain the uneasiness she felt. "And the gifts must show thankfulness for and give blessing to the receiver. Uncle says that is the most important part of the tradition." Elizabeth folded the cloth, smoothed it and placed it on top of her work basket. "I know giving of a neckcloth may appear improper, but I do owe him one. Had he not ruined his when tending to my wound, I may not be here to give any gifts. The doctor did say the binding probably saved my life. How can I show my gratitude if I do not replace it?"

"Oh, Elizabeth," cried Georgiana. "You have nothing to fear. Do you think we adhere to the utmost propriety at all times? Have you not met Richard?" She laughed lightly. "Fitzwilliam will love your gifts." She tucked the handkerchief she had been working on in her workbasket closing it securely in preparation for leaving. "We must be at Matlock House within the hour. Aunt Elaine is most particular about promptness."

Elizabeth picked up her parcels and headed for the carriage. "I have a gift for your aunt, Georgiana. I hate to tell you, but I am nervous about it, too." Elizabeth attempted to laugh at her own foolishness. "I am not certain when I decided to pick up a case of my mother's nerves, but I seem to have come down with the affliction as of late. I suppose I must be thankful it has not been accompanied by her fluttering about." Elizabeth once again attempted to laugh to assuage the tension she was feeling. "My uncle helped me pick out some teas, and Aunt Gardiner, Jane, and I made some sweets. It is rather a homey gift and not exactly elegant. It is something that I would give to my aunts. Do you think its simplicity will offend her?" Again, Elizabeth chewed her lip.

"Elizabeth, you protect your cousin with your life, talk circles around Miss Bingley, and tease my dour brother, yet a gift makes you quake? Your lack of confidence surprises me," chided Georgiana as the carriage jostled along the streets. "I have stitched a cloth for my aunt's table. It is a homey sort of gift just like yours and exactly what she would like."

Elizabeth looked chagrinned. "I shall try to compose myself and stop acting so foolishly. I have always prided myself on my courage rising to meet all situations, yet here I sit a ball of nerves."

Georgiana patted Elizabeth's hand. "All will be well. You know, Uncle Henry and Aunt Elaine are quite taken with your uncle's gift giving tradition. I believe Aunt Elaine sees it for what it is, but Uncle seems to think it could be a boon of an idea for merchants." She smiled at Elizabeth. "Yes, I know it is not proper for a lady to know of business dealing, but I have already told you, my family is not always so proper. Uncle was quite worked up about it the other evening when talking to my brother. He was quite put out that your uncle will not hear of advertising the concept. He is constantly looking for new ways to increase profits, you see."

"Is he angry with my uncle?" Elizabeth's eyes were filled with concern.

"No, no, he is not angry with him. He gets overwrought with excitement at times and relies on people such as my brother and your uncle to guide him, so he does not jump into any venture without due consideration. He is never happy to have his ideas thwarted, but as I said, he trusts the judgement of his counsellors. I believe he agrees with your uncle that such a decision should not be made in haste, that there is a need to protect the sentiment behind the tradition." Georgiana peered out the window and then turned to Elizabeth with a smile. "Now, take a deep breath; we are almost there, and remember, she likes you."

Elizabeth nodded and inhaled deeply. She leaned her head back against the squabs and closed her eyes. She knew that she had nothing to fear, but she had fallen short of her mother's expectations for so many years that it only seemed natural to expect to do so again.

Georgiana gently tapped Elizabeth's arm as the carriage came to a stop. "We are here."

~*~*~*~*~*~

Lady Matlock stood and extended her hands in greeting to Mrs. Gardiner and Jane. "It is a pleasure to have you join me for tea."

She turned to Georgiana and Elizabeth and welcomed them both, to Elizabeth's surprise, with a hug. "Georgiana, Miss Elizabeth, you are both looking well today."

"Thank you, Aunt," murmured Georgiana.

"Thank you, my lady," said Elizabeth still somewhat surprised over the familiar greeting.

Lady Matlock motioned for them to take a seat.

"Georgiana, your brother is stopping by a little later." Lady Matlock began to pour the tea. "He has some business with your Uncle." She handed a cup to Mrs. Gardiner. "But I think he may actually be trying to get a peek at his gift, although, I am sure that is not the only reason he intends to drop by today." She shared a knowing smile with Mrs. Gardiner.

"I should think not," said Mrs. Gardiner.

Elizabeth's cheeks grew warm. "Lady Matlock, as we are talking about presents, I have a small gift for you," said Elizabeth holding out the package that she held in her lap. "My uncle helped me select part of it and my aunt and Jane helped me with the rest." She unconsciously bit her lower lip.

Lady Matlock noted the nervous action and smiled at her. "Thank you. May I open it now, or do I have to wait?"

"I think it would be best to open it now as it may not survive waiting," said Elizabeth.

"Oh," gasped Lady Matlock in delight as she opened the gift. "Your uncle has done well in his advice. These are some of my favourite teas, and is this chocolate conserves? I have a sweet tooth that is exceptionally fond of chocolate." She picked up a piece and took a small bite. "You made this?" she asked as she took a second bite.

"Yes, Elizabeth made the chocolate conserves, Jane and I made the shortbreads," said Mrs. Gardiner.

"Miss Elizabeth, you seem to have a talent for confections. I have never tasted such lovely conserves, and I do not exaggerate. Georgiana, you may have to ask her to make you some for I do not know if I shall be sharing." She took a second piece and placed it on the edge of her saucer.

"Thank you," said Elizabeth. "Conserves are a specialty for me simply because I seem to lack the patience to wait for shortbreads to bake."

Tea was served and the ladies chatted about the weather, their plans for travel, and the traditions of Christmas in each of their homes. Lady Matlock shared stories of Georgiana, Darcy, and Richard as youngsters while Mrs. Gardiner shared about her nieces. They were sharing a good laugh when Darcy walked into the drawing room. He greeted each lady but in truth only had eyes for Elizabeth.

"I've come to see Uncle but wished to greet you first." He smiled broadly at his aunt. "Happily you were not alone."

"How very thoughtful of you, Fitzwilliam." His aunt gave him with a knowing smile. "Miss Elizabeth, I shall have to share your gift with my nephew. He is not as great a lover of sweets as I am, but like me, he has a weakness for conserves. Now, take a piece for yourself and one for your uncle, and make sure the second piece actually makes it to your uncle. Miss Elizabeth made it and included it with some lovely shortbreads and a selection of my favourite teas."

"I think you are becoming a favourite of my aunt's, Miss Elizabeth."

"Oh, now get away with you." Lady Matlock made a shooing motion. "Your uncle is waiting."

"I shan't be long. Georgiana, will you wait?"

"Elizabeth and I had not planned to leave before dinner." She raised an eyebrow at her brother. "You have not forgotten we were to dine here tonight, have you?" There was a hint of incredulity in her voice.

Darcy grinned. "I have not forgotten. I merely wished to be assured I would have pleasant company awaiting me after my meeting with Uncle." He gave his sister a small wink, and with a last loving look at Elizabeth, exited the room.

"Mr. Bingley is joining us for dinner this evening, and I have a few preparations to attend to before his arrival." Mrs. Gardiner and Jane rose to take their leave. "It has been a pleasure. I have not enjoyed myself this much in a very long time, Lady Matlock."

"You shall have to call again, Mrs. Gardiner. It was a lovely time." Lady Matlock stood to walk her guests to the door.

"Aunt," said Elizabeth. "Mr. Thompson called on Andrew. I shall walk you to the carriage and relay his message if that is acceptable." She looked first to Lady Matlock and then her aunt for permission before escorting her aunt and sister from the room.

"Miss Elizabeth is lovely, is she not, Georgiana?" Lady Matlock watched Elizabeth from the window.

"Quite lovely, Aunt. I should be extremely pleased to have her for a sister."

"And I would very much like to have her for a niece, so we must make sure your brother succeeds." Lady Matlock arranged herself in her chair once more, making sure to smooth her skirts so that they were displayed to best advantage. "Do you know much about Miss Lucas?"

"She is quite lovely as well. She is practical and intelligent. Did you know she has studied herbal preparations? It was she who assisted with the closure of both Andrew's and Elizabeth's wounds, and Elizabeth credits Miss Lucas' tea for keeping infection away while she and her cousin were recovering. Why do you ask?"

"I noticed Richard paying particular attention to her on the evening before she left."

Elizabeth smiled as she slipped into her seat. "I assume you are speaking of Charlotte?" she asked quietly.

"Yes, I was just asking Georgiana if she could give me some information about the type of lady that Miss Lucas is, but you might be better able to assist me."

"I have known Charlotte all my life, my lady, so

I may not be the most objective source of information."

"I disagree. I believe you would be a perfect person to tell me about her. You strike me as a very honest individual. I would not doubt anything you would tell me."

"I am honoured to be thought of so highly." Elizabeth paused for a moment, remembering what Darcy had told her about Richard's concern about his parents' acceptance of Miss Lucas. Carefully she considered what information the mother of a gentleman might wish to know about the lady who had captured his attentions. "I shall tell you what I can. She is the eldest child of Sir William Lucas, whom you have met. He is both a landowner and a merchant. He made his wealth first through trade. Now, he holds his store for the sole purpose of providing an additional source of income for the inheritance of those children who are not his heir. Charlotte has three brothers and one sister. You have met Maria. Her brothers are Jacob, the oldest and heir, Matthew and Elijah.

"Charlotte has an adequate dowry for her station in life, but I am not supposed to know about it. I happened to overhear the information, and cannot in good conscience tell you more than that. In fact, I have not even told Charlotte what I know. She will also have a portion of either the sale of her father's store or a small annual income from the store upon her father's death. Matthew will inherit the running of the store if he wishes to claim it, with the stipulation of the incomes for Charlotte, Maria and Elijah." Elizabeth hoped that this information would allay some of Lady Matlock's concerns. However, she was sure there were more questions to be answered, and she waited patiently.

Lady Matlock tipped her head slightly to one side. "And her character, Miss Elizabeth, what is her character like?"

Elizabeth smiled. It appeared Lady Matlock had accepted Charlotte's connections if she were now inquiring about her character. "She is loyal and loving though she is not a romantic. Her goal in life is to have a home of her own, a comfortable situation. Although she would like to marry for love, she is, as she says, sensible enough to know that such arrangements are not available for everyone, and she will make her choice for practical reasons. She has no wish to be a burden to her family."

Lady Matlock prepared to ask a further question, but a commotion in the front hall forestalled it.

"I must see my brother," came a loud and angry voice.

"Oh, dear," said Lady Matlock. "I fear we are about to be fortunate enough to be visited by Lady Catherine, Georgiana."

"Elaine, where is Henry? I must speak with Henry this instant on business which cannot be delayed," said Lady Catherine entering the drawing room.

"He is in his study — in a meeting. Would you like some tea while you wait?" said Lady Matlock.

"No, I could not possibly enjoy tea right now. My nerves are in such a state." As she turned to take a seat, her eyes locked onto Elizabeth. "Are you Elizabeth Bennet?" she asked.

"I am."

"Good. I would also like to speak with you."

"Me? To what may I ascribe this honour?" Elizabeth asked suspiciously.

"A report of a most alarming nature reached me two days ago. I was told that not only is your sister Mary on the point of being most advantageously married, but that you would in all likelihood be following her. I have come to ascertain the veracity of this report. Is it true, Miss Elizabeth, that you are to wed my nephew, Fitzwilliam Darcy?"

"And from whom have you received this report, Lady Catherine?"

"I have had it from not one but two sources. One is your own cousin, Mr. Collins, and the other is a friend of yours from London, a Miss Bingley." Lady Catherine had found the largest remaining seat in the room and perched herself upon it.

"And how do these sources claim to have come across this information?" Elizabeth struggled to keep the indignation out of her voice. A harsh answer would not serve in this situation.

"Why from your father and you," said Lady Catherine with a huff. "I would like you to verify that their reports are false as I know they must be since my nephew is engaged to my daughter, Anne."

"If you suppose the report to be false, I do not see why you would go to the trouble of travelling to London to question me about it." Elizabeth continued quickly cutting off any response Lady Catherine was about to make, "If Mr. Darcy is indeed engaged to your daughter, I would think that you would trust his honour in fulfilling his commitment. However, if you doubt his honour, I wonder why you would allow your daughter to be engaged to him in the first place." This comment drew a gasp from Georgiana and a pleased smile from Lady Matlock.

Lady Catherine was not pleased. "This will not do. I will not have it. Are you, Miss Bennet, engaged to my nephew? I must know the truth," bellowed Lady Catherine.

"He has not spoken to my father," said Elizabeth softly.

"And will you promise to never enter into an arrangement with him?"

"I did not say I did not have an understanding with him, Lady Catherine." She was no longer able to keep the anger out of her voice. "I only said he has not spoken to my father. What I may or may not have agreed to when speaking with your nephew is of no importance to you."

"Such insolence is not to be borne! I shall know how to act," screeched Lady Catherine. "Do not think that Mr. Collins will be allowed to marry your sister and remain comfortably situated at

Hunsford if you persist in practicing your arts and enticements that have ensnared my nephew. No, it would not be proper for me to lend my support to a clergyman who insists on being associated with such a woman. Indeed, your reputation will throw disparagement on his authority within his congregation. Should the bishop hear of such a thing, he will surely look on it with displeasure!"

"You would not!" gasped Elizabeth.

"I would, and I shall. Would you be so selfish as to damage the hopes of your family? Loss of such a connection in regards to the entail on your father's estate would be devastating. Do you think your sister will persist in this engagement once the misery of her situation is made clear to her? And what of your reputation and that of your family when your shameful pursuit and entrapment of a husband is made known?" Lady Catherine stepped menacingly toward Elizabeth.

"What is going on in here?" roared Lord Matlock.

"I am here to protect Anne's position, Henry. This..." Lady Catherine poked a gnarled finger at Elizabeth. "This adventuress has tricked our nephew into forgetting about his familial duty."

Darcy pushed into the room and positioned himself between his aunt and Elizabeth. He glowered at Lady Catherine, "You shall not speak to her so."

"See he forgets his place." She waved her hand in dismissal of Darcy's words.

"He has forgotten nothing, Catherine," said Lord Matlock firmly. "The engagement between Anne and Darcy exists only in your mind."

"It does not. Darcy's mother and I have always spoken of it," retorted Lady Catherine.

Lord Matlock stepped within inches of his sister and lowered his voice though it lost none of its displeasure. "No, you spoke of it, and no one spoke against you. There is a difference. Darcy is free to choose where he sees fit. He has no obligation to you or Anne. You will cease to speak of this foolishness, and you will insult Miss Elizabeth no longer. Do I make myself clear?"

"You will regret this, Henry!" Lady Catherine spun to look at Elizabeth. "So will you! Do not think your sister will not feel the regret of your decision." She wagged a finger at Darcy. "You, disregarding duty for a pretty..."

Darcy took a threatening step towards her.

"Take care, Aunt." There was no mistaking the warning in his voice.

"Your mother would be very disappointed, very disappointed indeed." With that, she stomped out of the room.

The colour drained from Elizabeth's face, and she slumped down into her chair. Darcy looked first at Elizabeth and then at his sister and aunt. "What does she mean your sister will feel the regret?" he asked.

"Mary," Elizabeth began to explain, but the words caught in her throat with a sob, and she shook her head.

Darcy looked again at his aunt for an explanation, but instead it was Georgiana who spoke. "As you know, Elizabeth's sister Mary is engaged to Mr. Collins. Aunt Catherine is threatening to make life decidedly uncomfortable for Mary if she insists on going through with the marriage. She has threatened to speak to the bishop about the living being removed from Mr. Collins ."

"I will send an express to your father," began Lord Matlock. "He must receive all correspondence that enters his home. Catherine must not be able to contact Mr. Collins. I will also speak to her staff, perhaps they can redirect any messages to me before they are posted." He paced the room. "I am sorry, Miss Elizabeth, that my sister has chosen to be so vicious."

He came to a stop at the door to the drawing room. "Mitchell," he called to his butler. "Please notify my solicitor that I need to see him within the hour on urgent business."

He turned back to the room. "I believe it is time for Catherine to hand over the running of Rosings to her daughter. I will not allow her to return to her home if she follows through on her threats. I will see to the express now." He walked over to his wife and whispered in her ear before he left the room.

Lady Matlock rose and motioned for Georgiana to follow her. She gave Darcy a smile and nodded in Elizabeth's direction before firmly closing the doors to the drawing room. Darcy needed no further invitation. He swiftly gathered Elizabeth into his arms and held her close. "All will be well," he whispered. The emotions that Elizabeth had been fighting finally broke through, and she wept on his shoulder. "All will be well, my love," he whispered once again.

"I want to believe it, Fitzwilliam. I truly do."

She took the handkerchief he offered and dried her tears. "It has to be well. I cannot live with myself if I am the cause of my sister's misery, nor can I live without you. It must be well for I cannot make such a decision. I will not make such a decision."

A soft knock sounded at the door. "Brother?" called Georgiana.

Darcy led Elizabeth to a chair and made sure of her comfort before opening the door.

"Dinner will be delayed until after Uncle has spoken to his solicitor. Aunt is packing and wishes for you to notify Bingley that she and Uncle will be travelling to Hertfordshire with us."

"But, you mustn't tell him why." Elizabeth's voice was filled with panic. "Georgiana, remember what Lady Catherine said about her sources of information?"

"Right. Miss Bingley was one of them."

"Miss Bingley?"

"Oh!" Elizabeth stood and paced a few steps before turning to Darcy. "If Miss Bingley speaks to Mr. Collins, he will know of his patroness' displeasure, and all of your uncle's efforts will be undone. I will lose you." The tears began to roll down her cheeks once more.

Darcy pulled Elizabeth into his embrace once again. "You will not lose me, Elizabeth, for I cannot live without you." He tipped her chin up so that he could look into her eyes. "I love you more than life itself, Elizabeth Bennet. You shall be my wife." He bent to give her a kiss. Georgiana quietly stepped out of the room and closed the door.

"Is Fitzwilliam within?" asked Lady Matlock. "I must speak to him about our travel arrangements."

Georgiana stood in front of the doors to the drawing room her hands remained firmly on the handles. "Yes, he is within, but I would not disturb him right now. Perhaps in a few moments it might be wise to interrupt him, but I would knock first."

"Oh?" Lady Matlock raised her eyebrows.

"Elizabeth is quite distraught, and he is, um, comforting her," Georgiana explained, her eyes focused on the floor in front of her and a faint blush colouring her cheeks. "She is afraid Miss Bingley will say something to Mr. Collins and all of Uncle's efforts will be in vain, and she will lose Fitzwilliam."

"Lose Fitzwilliam?" her aunt repeated incredulously.

"I do not think she will marry him if it means

harming her sister," said Georgiana softly. "And if she does not marry him, Aunt, after what I have witnessed, I fear for them both. Their devastation would be complete." Tears stung the corners of Georgiana's eyes.

"Oh, dear, I knew she was devoted to those she loved. After all, she did place herself in the path of a bullet to protect her cousin. This is not good, Georgiana. Go tell your uncle to include in his express that no correspondence of any sort is to be delivered to Mr. Collins until after he and I arrive in Hertfordshire."

Georgiana scooted down the hall to her uncle's study.

Lady Matlock stepped to the door and knocked. She smiled as she heard a quick shuffling inside the room. Patiently, she waited for Darcy to open the door.

Chapter 10

"Good morning, Miss Bennet, Miss Elizabeth," greeted Lord Matlock as they stood in front of the Gardiner's home waiting for the last trunk to be secured to the Gardiner's carriage. "I pray you are in better spirits this morning, Miss Elizabeth."

"I am, thank you, but might I have a word with you in private?"

"Certainly." Lord Matlock extended his arm and the two of them began to stroll up the street a short distance.

"I was thinking." She looked away from Lord Matlock and drew a breath as if gathering her courage. "What if I break off my courtship with Mr. Darcy, for now—to give Lady Catherine and Miss Bingley the appearance that they are succeeding? This would then give my sister a chance to marry, and perhaps with your help and that of Mr.

Darcy, we could find another parish for my cousin. One where he and my sister could be comfortable and perhaps even within a reasonable distance from my mother." Again she drew a breath to steady her nerves. "After Mr. Collins is in possession of such an income, Mr. Darcy and I would be free to resume our courtship. I know it is a bit of subterfuge, and normally, I abhor all forms of deceit, but I can think of no other way to avoid hurting someone for whom I truly care." Elizabeth looked at Lord Matlock, her eyes filled with disquiet.

Lord Matlock considered her, a gentle smile on his face. "Yours is not a plan without merit." He patted her arm. "I shall keep it in mind; however, I think we can get both you and your sister married without the interference of either my sister or Bingley's. Will you trust me?"

"Will you use my plan if yours does not work?"

"I will."

"Then, I will trust you." She paused, drew in another deep breath and looked into Lord Matlock's eyes. "I love him, sir. With every ounce of my being, I love him, and I will do whatever you require not to lose him."

Lord Matlock's eyes shimmered. "I understand, Miss Elizabeth. You shall not lose him," he promised.

"Thank you, sir. I shall hold you to your word."

Lord Matlock laughed softly. "I would expect no less, Miss Elizabeth. And how can I fail when I would have to answer to both you and my wife if I do? It is great motivation, my dear, for I do not wish to disappoint either of you." He covered Elizabeth's hand with his. "Now, if I do not return you to Darcy soon, he shall be after me."

"I fear you are too late, my lord." Elizabeth leaned closer and spoke softly, giving a nod in the direction of Darcy, who strode towards them with very determined steps.

"Bingley is here," Darcy said as he approached. "He is only joined by his sister Louisa and her husband. Miss Bingley has decided, with her brother's help, that remaining in town to enjoy the many events of the season would be more beneficial to her than coming to Netherfield."

"She will remain here alone?" asked Elizabeth.

"No, Bingley's aunt and uncle from Scarborough will be joining her. Apparently, they had planned to come to town for the holidays, and their arrival presented a convenient way for Miss Bingley to remain in town."

Elizabeth arched her eyebrow and tilted her head as she looked at Lord Matlock suspiciously. "Part of your plan?" she asked.

"Most definitely," he said with a pleased smile. "Now, shall we depart? Richard plans to join us in a few days. Do you think Miss Lucas will mind having him in Meryton for the holidays?"

"Not in the least, my lord, not in the least," replied Elizabeth with a little laugh.

~*~*~*~*~*~

At the last carriage stop, seats were rearranged at Lord Matlock's insistence. "I assume this is another part of your plan." Elizabeth settled into the comfortable seat in Lord Matlock's carriage. "It would not do to have Mr. Darcy delivering me to my father's house with Mr. Collins present, now would it?"

Lord Matlock shook his head. "Miss Elizabeth, your perception amazes me. I did not wish for Mr. Collins to witness the friendship that you and Darcy have established until I had first had time to meet him and your father. Now, tell me more about your family. I want a good lay of the land, so to speak, before embarking on our campaign in earnest."

Elizabeth and Jane spent much of the remaining journey describing their home, their sisters and their parents to Lord and Lady Matlock.

"You may completely change your mind about my suitability for your nephew once you have met them." Elizabeth laughed nervously.

"Could they be any worse than my sister?" asked Lord Matlock.

"You have a point, sir. It seems neither of us is without embarrassing relatives. However, I have only met one such relative of yours, and you are about to meet several of mine."

"Do not fret. I assure you I have many more embarrassing relatives for you to meet at a later date, but to ensure that you marry my nephew, I shan't introduce you to them until after the wedding."

"You are assuming that my father will give his blessing, sir," teased Elizabeth.

"Indeed I am. How very forward of me. Will you accept my apologies?" Lord Matlock said with feigned gravity.

"But, of course, my lord," said Elizabeth just as

the carriages pulled into the circular drive in front of Longbourn.

Mr. and Mrs. Bennet and their daughters along with Mr. Collins stood on the front steps to meet them. The Gardiners were first out of their carriage. As the Bennets and Gardiners gave each other hugs and handshakes, Lord Matlock handed his wife and then Jane and Elizabeth out of his carriage.

Mr. Bennet approached his daughters and Elizabeth stepped forward to give him a hug. "Lord and Lady Matlock, may I introduce my father, Mr. Bennet. Father, the Earl and Countess of Matlock."

"Welcome to Longbourn, Lord and Lady Matlock. I trust your trip was pleasant."

"It was quite pleasant," said Lord Matlock. "You are blessed with two very fine daughters Mr. Bennet, travelling with them has been most enjoyable."

"Thank you for delivering them to me, my lord. Would you care to come in for some refreshment before heading to Netherfield?" inquired Mr. Bennet.

"We would be happy to," said Lady Matlock.

Once inside the house, Lord and Lady Matlock

were introduced to the rest of the Bennet family and Mr. Collins. To Elizabeth's amazement, Mrs. Bennet greeted her guests with reserved dignity.

"This is a charmingly situated room, Mrs. Bennet," said Lady Matlock.

"Thank you, my lady," said Mrs. Bennet. "It is situated quite nicely to take advantage of all the sun available in the dreary winter months. Yet it catches the prevailing breezes in the summer and is shaded by the trees which stand in the side garden."

Elizabeth handed Lady Matlock a cup of tea prepared just as her ladyship liked it. She took a sip and smiled in appreciation of Elizabeth's efforts.

"I have come to enjoy the company of your daughters, Mrs. Bennet. They and Mrs. Gardiner joined me for tea just yesterday when we were in town, and we have shared at least one evening in company." Lady Matlock paused to sip her tea. "I understand you have a daughter who is soon to be wed. Which one is she?"

"Mary dear, come here. Lady Matlock wishes to meet you," Mrs. Bennet called. "And bring Mr. Collins with you."

"Lord Matlock, Gardiner has just delivered a

fine bottle of port. Would you care to help us inspect its quality?" asked Mr. Bennet.

The men retired to the library while the women and Mr. Collins remained in the parlour where talk focused on the upcoming wedding.

"I have a few pieces of correspondence that have come for Mr. Collins. They are here." Mr. Bennet reached into a drawer of his desk, drew out two envelopes and handed them to Lord Matlock. "I do not fully understand why I was to keep his correspondence and give it to you instead of him, but I have done as you requested."

"I am glad that you have. It seems I have a prob-lem with my sister, Lady Catherine, and he is her parson. She has always held to the idea that one day Darcy and her daughter, Anne, would marry. This has never been true and the supposition regarding their engagement is merely a figment of her imagination. In fact, Darcy's father made it clear to me that he did not wish for his son to marry his cousin Anne. Of course, if they were truly in love, he would have supported the match. How-ever, they are not now and never have been. I should not be the one to tell you this perhaps, but my nephew's heart is engaged elsewhere although he has not yet had the opportunity to speak to the lady's father." Matlock gave a small nod of acknowledgment in answer to Mr. Bennet's questioning look before taking a sip of his port. "Ah, Gardiner, you do know your port," he said with appreciation.

"And what does all of this have to do with Mr. Collins' correspondence?" inquired Mr. Bennet.

"Well, it seems my sister has been made aware of my nephew's growing attachment to your daughter, and one of her sources is Mr. Collins. I have been led to believe that Mr. Collins esteems his patroness very highly and will bow to her every request."

"That is true, my lord," agreed Mr. Bennet.

"Just Matlock, please," said Lord Matlock with a smile. "Yesterday, Catherine came to my house to demand that Darcy marry her daughter. Unfortunately, your daughter was calling on my wife at the time. Catherine made her request to your daughter. Elizabeth is not one to be backed into a corner very easily, Bennet. She is quite remarkable actually." He paused to enjoy more of his port.

"To come to the point, Catherine has threatened to not allow Mr. Collins to marry your other daughter Mary and still comfortably retain his position at Hunsford should Elizabeth come to any sort of understanding with Darcy. I am sure you are aware that Elizabeth will not marry Darcy if it means harming her sister." Mr. Bennet's brows rose in surprise at this news. "She has told me as much. I believe that once you have seen her in company with my nephew, you will agree that for them not to marry would be a grave misfortune. Am I not correct, Gardiner?"

"He speaks the truth, Bennet."

"I knew from your letter, Gardiner, that there was a fondness, but it has really grown to this?"

"Indeed, it has, brother. And a finer match could not be found for our Lizzy."

"Or Darcy," added Matlock. "So our purpose is to keep Catherine from speaking to Mr. Collins until after he and Mary are married. Since Catherine's daughter Anne is of age to claim her inheritance, I have taken steps to remove Catherine from Rosings completely. She shall not have control over any aspect of the estate unless Anne allows it. This should limit her ability to make life miserable for Mr. and Mrs. Collins. I have also put about to my connections regarding an alternate living for Mr. Collins should Hunsford not remain an advantageous option for him. And while I am here, I hope to sway his allegiance away from Catherine and toward me as I am the head of the family."

"That is a tall order, Matlock. I do hope you are up to the challenge. Mr. Collins is not the most intelligent of men," warned Mr. Bennet. "I would not have consented to Mary's marriage except for the fact that she truly seems happy with him." Mr. Bennet shook his head as if he still could not believe that anyone could be happy to be married to Mr. Collins.

"I have been given an alternate plan, Bennet, should my plan fail," said Matlock.

Mr. Bennet raised his eyebrows. "Lizzy?"

Lord Matlock nodded. "Your daughter has suggested she break off her courtship with my nephew and face the derision and unhappiness that such a choice would bring. With this goal in mind, she has asked me to find an alternate living for him. A wedding can happen quickly, but the search for a living within a reasonable distance from Longbourn could take some time. Once the wedding has taken place and Mr. Collins is installed in such a living, she would then be more than happy to reinstate her courtship with Darcy. It is not a plan that I wish to implement as I know the heartache that would come to both Darcy and Elizabeth. However, she has made me promise I would consider it."

"It is hard not to listen to her when she is bent on a purpose, is it not?" chuckled Mr. Bennet. "I would not like to see us have to resort to her plan either unless we are at the end of all other options."

"Darcy does not know about Elizabeth's plan," said Matlock, "and I will not tell him of it unless we need to employ it."

"I understand, Matlock. Not a word of the plan will cross my lips," Mr. Bennet assured Lord Matlock.

~*~*~*~*~*~

Elizabeth stood outside her father's study looking at the woman in front of her. She looked like Mary, but she did not act like Mary. Mary had always been quiet and solemn, almost mousy. This woman had just demonstrated an ability to charm her betrothed with the bat of an eyelash better than Lydia could ever have done, and now she was leading her sister into the conference going on inside the study with the command of a general.

"Elizabeth, all will be well," said Mary. "I really must speak to father and Lord Matlock immediately. I cannot tell you why while we are standing here. It is not safe. Trust me." With that, she rapped firmly on the study door and waited. When Mr. Gardiner opened the door, she grabbed Elizabeth's wrist and dragged her into the room pushing past her uncle in her haste.

"Mary," said her father in surprise. "What are you doing here?" He looked at Elizabeth, who just shrugged her shoulders and rubbed her wrist.

"I have something that you and Lord Matlock must know," said Mary curtseying to Lord Matlock. "I assume you are discussing Lady Catherine?" she continued. The men looked at her in surprise.

"Lady Catherine?" said Elizabeth suspiciously.

"Yes, Elizabeth. I have met Lady Catherine, but two days before your arrival."

"Lady Catherine was here?" questioned Mr. Bennet. "Why do I not know of this?"

"Mother had taken Kitty and Lydia to town. Remember, Papa, they are not allowed to travel to town by themselves since...." she looked at Elizabeth but did not finish the sentence. "You and Mr.

Collins were out for a ride about the estate. I alone was here to greet her."

"What did my sister have to say to you?" asked Matlock.

"A considerable amount, my lord, but to sum up the conversation, she tried to get me to answer questions about Lizzy and Mr. Darcy. I did not have the information she sought. She then tried to get me to promise to dissuade Lizzy from ever accepting Mr. Darcy. I could not. She then told me that I would be miserable as mistress of Hunsford if I did not reconsider and assist her in this matter. She informed me that she would be in communication soon with Mr. Collins after a quick trip to London.

"I assume, Lord Matlock, that you have come to Longbourn to discuss a plan which will allow both my sister and me the freedom to marry as we choose?"

"Your daughters, Bennet, are extremely adept at putting together facts and coming up with correct assessments," said Matlock with a chuckle. "Yes, Miss Mary, I am here to discuss how we can protect both you and Miss Elizabeth."

"Good," said Mary. "I have a plan."

"Another daughter with a plan?" said Mr. Bennet. "How ever did you all become so conniving?"

"Have you met our mother?" said Mary with an impertinent grin, sending a ripple of laughter around the room.

"Yes, I believe I have had the good fortune of meeting the woman," said her father. "So, Mary, what is your plan? Lord Matlock has already shared Elizabeth's plan with me."

"I believe we should move up the date of the wedding," stated Mary. "I am sure that I can convince Mr. Collins that it would be an excellent idea since such an illustrious member of his patroness' family is here as a representative to give their blessing to the union. Once we are married, we will only need to deal with the living at Hunsford." She moved to stand next to her father.

"I believe that Lady Catherine's daughter has reached her majority, has she not? I also understand that eventually she shall be mistress of Rosings in her mother's stead. Could we not assist her in assuming her rightful role?" She circled the room. "Then, Lady Catherine's influence may not be felt as strongly, allowing Mr. Collins and me to reside in relative comfort. And perhaps, there might be some agreeable young men we could present to Miss de Bourgh as possible suitors. She cannot marry Mr. Darcy if she marries someone else, now can she?" She stood near Elizabeth, her hands on her hips looking very determined.

"Who are you?" asked Elizabeth.

"I am your sister Mary," said Mary taking Elizabeth's hand. "I have just found my voice is all. I realize that the seemingly scheming nature of this plan does not coexist readily in your mind with the picture of the moralizing sister I have always been."

"Indeed, it does not."

Mary held both of Elizabeth's hands securely and looked her in the eyes. "But, Elizabeth, it would not be right to stand aside and allow Lady Catherine to continue in her unkind and controlling manner. Providence has brought Mr. Collins and me together as well as you and Mr. Darcy. It would be unconscionable to allow any man or woman to work so forcefully against the designs of the Almighty and to do so in such an unchristian fashion."

Matlock laughed. "Miss Mary, I quite enjoy your straightforward approach to the situation. You do not mince words. But, it will still be possible for my sister to make life miserable for you at Hunsford."

"I am aware of that. Does she not have a house in town to which she can be removed if she were to be too much of an interference? I have not met Miss de Bourgh, but I have heard she has a fragile constitution. It might actually be best for Miss de Bourgh to have some time without her mother when she is assuming the role of mistress. I can well imagine how a mother's presence could be overwhelming and cause a great deal of stress to her daughter."

Mr. Bennet snorted.

"Your points are valid. I could ask Darcy, Richard or my eldest son, Thaddeus, to assist Anne in her new position. Of course, my wife would also wish to help her with those things of which the men may not be aware and to provide the proper appearance of a chaperone."

"Then it is settled, gentlemen." Mary smiled widely. "I will speak to Mr. Collins about the wedding date while you, Lord Matlock, continue to move Rosings from Lady Catherine's possession to that of her daughter. Papa, your job is to speak to Mr. Darcy and Mr. Bingley and give them your blessing. Mr. Gardiner, you must see to it that my mother is kept unaware of the circumstances of which we have been speaking."

"And what shall I do?" asked Elizabeth.

"You," said Mary with a magnanimous smile, "have the hardest task of all. You and Mr. Darcy shall do nothing." She looked to Lord Matlock, who vigorously nodded his approval. "I shall need you and Jane to be my support and deal with our younger sisters, but other than that you shall do nothing. I am sure your plan was a good one, but I am just as sure that your plan would have left you with a far greater wound than the one that scars your arm. I am also sure your plan put my desires and wishes before your own. You have always protected me as much as you were able while we were growing up. It is time, Elizabeth, to let me do this for you. Allow me, Papa, Lord Matlock, and Uncle Gardiner to protect you from injury. Can you do that?"

Tears stung at the corners of Elizabeth's eyes. "I can try," she said.

Chapter 11

"Anne, what brings you to Matlock House?" Thaddeus stood as she entered the drawing room.

"I had heard Richard intended to join your parents at Netherfield, and I was hoping I could go with him. Spending much more time with my mother will surely drive me to Bedlam," said Anne in exasperation.

"Is your mother still going on about Darcy?"

"Does she ever stop talking about Darcy?" Anne laughed. "I am tired to the point of weeping from hearing her carry on about our cousin. I have told her time and again that I do not wish to marry Darcy, but will she listen? No, her mind is set, and there seems to be no possible way of unsetting it." Anne dropped into a chair.

"She can be stubborn, but then again, it is a

Fitzwilliam trait, is it not?" Thaddeus offered his cousin a glass of wine.

"Indeed it is," said Anne. "I also wish to meet the lady who has captured our cousin's heart. I have heard only my mother's account of her, and I am sure my mother's description is far from the truth. Did you know that both this Miss Elizabeth and her sister, Miss Mary, who is to marry my mother's parson, stood up to my mother?" Thaddeus' eyes grew wide in astonishment.

Anne nodded. "Neither one would give her satisfaction, and it has her furious. Your father has effectively confined her to her townhouse by sending her carriage back to Rosings with strict instructions that it not be returned to London until he has sent for it." Anne settled back into her chair. "She will not be leaving town for some time, I should think. I do not see her reconciling herself to Darcy's marriage anytime in the near future. The vitriolic language I have endured since yesterday at this time when she came home from Matlock House has been shocking even for my mother. Thankfully, Mrs. Jennings and I were able to escape to come here."

"I have heard tell of battle lines being drawn,

and I have also heard some description of Darcy's lady from Richard. I think we would like her." Thaddeus cocked his head to the side and smiled. "Say, what if both you and I join Richard? I could use a bit of time out of town, and I would also like to meet this Miss Elizabeth Bennet."

"But, are you not to remain in town and procure a bride?" teased Anne. "Your mother is starting to despair of either of her boys ever giving her grandchildren."

"Ah, but I think Richard may assuage my mother's desires before me. I am safe for the time being. Besides, the women of the ton are shallow. I have yet to meet a genuine soul among them."

"Richard has his eye on someone?"

"He has not told me — not that I would expect him to — but he is selling out his commission and seems very eager to journey to Hertfordshire. It is my understanding Miss Elizabeth had friends visiting her while she was in London," explained Thaddeus. "Perhaps Hertfordshire is the new marriage market for those seeking sensible mates?"

"I wonder if it is only sensible females or if there are some sensible and marriageable males among the inhabitants of Hertfordshire?"

"Are you looking, too?" asked Thaddeus in surprise.

"Thad, I am not getting any younger, and I would like to get married someday—as long as it is not to Darcy."

"What is so wrong with Darcy?"

"There is nothing wrong with him. He is handsome and honourable and wealthy ..." Thaddeus snorted."...but he is Darcy. He and I have been thrown together since we were in leading strings. He is like a brother to me, and I would never be able to think of him as my husband." She shuddered at the thought.

Thaddeus laughed and looked at his pretty, delicate cousin. "So, no marrying of a cousin for you?"

"I did not say that." A slight blush graced her cheeks. "It would just have to be a cousin other than Darcy." She peered up at Thaddeus' handsome face through her lashes.

"Really? Perhaps I could help you find one?"

"If you wish," said Anne coyly.

"I do," said Thaddeus. "Helping you find a cousin to marry would be a pleasure." He took a step closer to her, but any further conversation was interrupted by the entrance of Richard.

"Well, it is done. I will be a free man shortly after Twelfth Night," he announced.

"So, you have sold out?" asked Thaddeus.

"I have indeed," said Richard. "Anne, it is good to see you." Richard moved across the room to her and gave her a kiss on the cheek. Thaddeus' eyes narrowed.

"Another who is like a brother," Anne reassured him softly. Richard looked at her quizzically.

"Anne was explaining to me how she could never marry Darcy since he was like a brother to her," explained Thaddeus as he poured a drink for his brother. "Richard, Anne would like to accompany you to Hertfordshire."

"What of your mother, Anne?" Richard took a seat across from her.

"What of her, cousin? I have had enough of her ranting to last me a lifetime. I wish to meet the subject of her rant, and Thaddeus has expressed a wish to join me on this adventure."

Richard blinked in surprise. "Thad, you want to leave town when there are so many social events happening?" Thaddeus had always enjoyed the crush of people and numerous young ladies who flocked to him at these events.

"I find I grow tired of my life as much as you grow tired of yours, brother," said Thaddeus with a raised eyebrow and a barely visible nod of his head in Anne's direction.

Richard's eyes narrowed questioningly, "Truly?"

"Yes, truly," said Thaddeus.

"Then I see no reason to not travel to Hertfordshire together. I planned to leave tomorrow morning. Will you be ready by then?"

"I am ready now," said Anne. "But morning does sound more sensible."

Richard laughed. "She is that bad, is she?"

"Worse," said Anne. "She can be so vindictive."

"You know, if you do not want to marry Darcy, you could marry someone else," said Richard.

Thaddeus glared at his brother before turning to refill his glass.

"If only I could get the right person to ask me," said Anne with a little laugh and a small motion of her head towards Thaddeus.

A knowing smile suffused Richard's face. "Well, I shall have to see what I can do about that," he whispered. Standing, he placed his empty glass on a table. "I think an express or two are in order.

One to Bingley and one to Darcy. I shall rejoin you before dinner. You are staying for dinner, are you not, Anne?"

"I would very much like to stay. I do not relish returning to my mother even for the night."

Richard looked to Mrs. Jenkins, who sat quietly in the corner stitching. "Mrs. Jenkins, are all of Anne's and your bags packed for the journey to Netherfield?"

"Yes, Colonel Fitzwilliam, they are." She looked up from her stitching, holding his gaze with her intelligent eyes. "They could be sent for if that is what you were thinking?" Her voice was soft but direct. "It would be easier to make our escape now than in the morning."

Richard chuckled. "That is exactly what I was thinking, Mrs. Jenkins, but you always have been able to assist me with my schemes without much prompting on my part. How do you do it?"

"You remind me of my younger brother, sir. I had to continually think three steps ahead to keep Thomas from trouble, but that is his wife's job now. God bless her." She chuckled softly. "Would you be so kind as to send a request for the delivery of our trunks, Colonel—since you will already be writing two other missives? Then, I can continue with this particularly trying bit of work." Her eyes darted toward her mistress and then Thad before she gave him a small wink and a smile. "I think I shall be able to accomplish much more here without Lady Catherine's interference," she added softly.

"Then it is settled. I will request your things be brought here so we might get an early start for Hertfordshire." He paused before he left to write his letters. "I think, madam, that one must stay more than three steps ahead of your scheming."

She simply raised an eyebrow while her lips curved slightly upward.

~*~*~*~*~*~

Darcy took a seat next to Elizabeth in Longbourn's sitting room. "Richard will arrive today, and he is bringing guests with him." He leaned a bit closer. "Thaddeus and Anne may be the answer to our problems."

"Thaddeus?" questioned Elizabeth.

"Thaddeus Herbert Oliver Fitzwilliam, Viscount Bladen is Richard's older brother," explained Darcy. He leaned just a little closer and whispered, "Richard seems to think there is a mutual interest between Thad and Anne."

"Truly?" Elizabeth's brows rose in surprise. "Mary had hinted we should find a suitor for Miss de Bourgh."

Darcy cocked his head to the side and drew his brows together. "Mary?"

"I believe her words were she cannot marry Mr. Darcy if she is already married to someone else, now can she?" Elizabeth laughed at the shocked look on Darcy's face. "No, she is not the same Mary we left a month ago. She has found her voice, and it is a rather take-charge voice, I am afraid. I was told in no uncertain terms that I am to leave the dealings with your aunt to my father, my uncle, your uncle and her."

"Did you have plans to deal with my aunt?"

Elizabeth bit her lip and studied her hands. "I spoke to your uncle about my plans before we left London."

"And were you ever going to inform me of these plans?" Darcy's voice was pained.

Elizabeth placed a hand on his arm. "I did not wish to tell you unless it became necessary, and your uncle assured me it would not as he was already working on a scheme." She withdrew her hand. "However, Mary has commandeered his plan and seems to be in charge. She will not even consider mine. In fact, she refuses to ask me what it is. She is under the impression that my idea would be too painful for the participants, and I would agree."

"So, you intended to break off your arrangement with me?" There was a hint of anger in his voice.

She nodded and her voice trembled just a bit. "I suggested I break off our courtship for the length of time necessary to get my sister married and a new living for her husband. Then, we would renew it." Elizabeth bit her lip and looked at Darcy with some trepidation in her eyes. "I love you. I could not...I would not give you up for good."

His voice softened. "But you also love your sister and could not be the cause of her disappointment?"

"Yes."

"I remember you saying something like that to me after my aunt's visit. I guess I should have been prepared for such a plan. You are not one to avoid injury to your person to secure the wellbeing of another."

"I am also not a person who will allow another to injure me without a fight, and I would fight for you with my last breath."

"I wish this room were not so full of people," whispered Darcy in a strained voice.

"It is rather crowded, is it not?" Elizabeth looked up at him through her lashes.

"Missa Dawcy, Missa Dawcy." Michael pulled on Darcy's coat.

Reluctantly, Darcy turned his eyes away from Elizabeth. "Yes, Master Michael?"

Michael's hands were filled with strings and blocks and sticks and cloth. "Boat, please?"

Darcy held out his hands, and Michael plopped his treasure into them before climbing into Darcy's lap. "I help," he stated.

Miss Lucy, the children's nursemaid, came rushing into the room. "Oh, thank heaven," she sighed when she saw Michael. "I am so sorry, sir. He said something about a boat and then escaped from the nursery at a fast pace."

"It is quite all right, Miss Lucy. We shall make a boat, and then I will deliver Master Michael back to your care." Miss Lucy curtseyed and returned to the nursery. "I imagine the children are getting as restless in the nursery as we are in the parlour," Darcy said to Elizabeth. "An outing might be a pleasant change. Hold this, Michael."

"And what do you have in mind?"

"I thought perhaps a walk around the garden or a carriage ride for a change of scene," said Darcy. "I even thought of asking Bingley if he would mind if we took them over to Netherfield and let them play in the nursery there.—May I have the sail, Michael?—It is opened up in anticipation of dinners and gatherings over the next few weeks."

As he talked, Darcy had been busy attaching sticks to blocks to fashion a crude boat, and with a final knot the sail stood in place. "There we are, Captain Michael. Now back to the nursery to defend your soldiers with such a nice ship." Michael smiled up at Darcy and slid to the floor taking Darcy by the hand. "Do you wish to accompany us into battle, Miss Elizabeth?"

Elizabeth laughed. "It would be my honour."

Chapter 12

"Mr. Darcy, do you know what you are taking upon yourself, sir?" Amusement tinged Mrs. Gardiner's her voice. "They can be a handful to maneuver even within the confines of a carriage."

"I believe I do."

"And I shall help him." Elizabeth leaned close to her aunt and whispered, "I also heard mention of a possible stop for some sweets in Meryton. It seems Mr. Darcy knows the value of a well-placed reward."

"Do not allow him to spoil them too much," said her aunt with a laugh as she turned to her children. "Michael, where are your gloves?" Michael spun on his heels and raced back to the nursery to retrieve the missing item. A few moments later, all the Gardiner children were waiting to climb into Mr. Darcy's carriage.

"Ladies," said Mr. Darcy with a bow, "may I hand you into the carriage?" The two young girls giggled and nodded. He extended his hand to each in turn calling them by name.

"Masters Michael and Andrew," Darcy motioned for the boys to enter the carriage. Michael required assistance, but Andrew refused, insisting he could do it himself.

"Miss Elizabeth?" said Darcy extending his hand to her.

"Thank you, Mr. Darcy." Elizabeth took his offered hand.

"Richard, would you care to join us?" asked Darcy.

"You said there would be sweets, right?"

"Only if you behave."

"Very well, I shall join you," said Richard, "but I am not promising to behave."

The three adults and four children squeezed onto the benches of the carriage.

"It is a very fine carriage," said Margaret. "The seats are so very comfortable."

"Thank you," said Darcy.

"We are very pleased to be joining you today, sir," said Amelia.

"I am very pleased you could join me."

"Sit down, Michael," scolded Elizabeth. Michael was standing on the seat between Richard and Darcy.

"I see?" he said with a pout as he slid down on the bench next to the gentlemen.

"Here," said Darcy picking him up and placing him on the side near the window while he slid over next to his cousin. "Now you can see, and you can sit so you will not get scolded."

"Thank you," said Michael.

"Darcy, I must say you have a way with children that completely baffles me," said Richard.

"I have been caring for my sister for some time," said Darcy. "These are not the first children with whom I have dealt; although, I am finding boys to be rather more fun than my sister."

"But she was twelve when we gained guardianship."

"But, she was only five when Mother died," said Darcy quietly. "Father was not himself after that, you know."

"Quite right," said Richard.

"I should not like to lose my mother or my

father," said Andrew. His sisters bobbed their heads in agreement.

"No one ever likes to lose someone they love," said Elizabeth. "Thankfully, it is not a path we walk down very often." Margaret grabbed Elizabeth's hand and gave it a squeeze. Darcy looked at her, his eyes filled with question. "I once had a brother, Mr. Darcy. His name was John."

"I am sorry. I had no idea."

"We do not speak of him often. Mama cannot bear it." She sighed. "It was an accident. A foolish accident." Margaret still held her hand, and Elizabeth placed her other hand over it welcoming the small bit of comfort it gave her. "Mama developed a dangerous fever near the time of her confinement — we thought we would lose her." She shook her head as if clearing away some of the memories. "As a result, John was born small and had a limping gait. The other boys made fun of him. I tried to always accompany him out, but on the day of the accident, Mama had some work for me to do, so I was unable to go with him. There is a wall on the eastern side of our estate that stands as tall as I am now. They dared him to walk along the top of it.

His weak leg gave out, and he fell. He was six. I was twelve at the time."

"So your protective nature was developed early," stated Richard. "Out of necessity to fend off your brother's tormentors."

"I believe my nature was there all along, but watching out for John strengthened it," agreed Elizabeth.

"And your competitive nature? Were you beating the boys before the accident?" asked Richard.

Elizabeth nodded. "I was, but not on such a consistent basis. I was quite determined to make them pay afterwards. And then, I discovered I was good at it, and I enjoyed it." Elizabeth laughed. "Now, I believe we were in the carriage to have a good time. Shall we play I spy?" Andrew clapped his hands, and Michael bounced on the seat. Elizabeth smiled at their exuberance. "Mr. Darcy, it is your carriage, so you must go first. What do you spy, sir?"

There were buttons and bows and trees that were spied as the carriage rolled along filled with giggling children and adults. Soon, they were in Meryton and a walk about the main street was proposed.

"Michael and Andrew, remember to hold a hand," cautioned Elizabeth. "Margaret and Amelia, stay close."

"Yes, Lizzy," sang out four young voices.

"I must say, Miss Elizabeth, you are a very capable commander," said Richard.

"Thank you, Colonel," said Elizabeth. "Now, take a hand." She pointed to Andrew, who was standing next to him.

"Yes, Miss Elizabeth," he said.

"And, Mr. Darcy, no carrying Michael for now. Those little legs need exercise before we make them sit still again."

"Yes, Miss Elizabeth." Darcy smiled. "Is she always so demanding?"

"Always," said Margaret. "But it is only to our benefit, Mr. Darcy."

"You are a wise young lady," complimented Darcy. "Shall we start at this shop and stop at all the windows? I think that shop across the street with the sweets shall be our last."

The group strolled down the street, peeping into windows to see what was being offered for sale. Richard would stop and squat down to see the items at a child-eye level and occasionally lift

Andrew to see something not visible from the child's vantage point. Of course, this meant Michael would also have to be lifted for he was not to be left out. Darcy listened carefully as the children expressed their admiration of various goods and made note of the preferred selection.

At last they came to the final store. It was a store which carried a variety of goods from food and sweets to tools and lace. It was a friendly store that welcomed a shopper upon entry.

"Good day, Miss Elizabeth," said the young gentleman behind the counter. "I see you have brought along several friends."

"Good day to you, Mr. Lucas. May I present Mr. Darcy and his cousin Colonel Fitzwilliam. Gentlemen, this is Mr. Matthew Lucas, second son of Sir William and Charlotte's younger brother. The children, Mr. Lucas, are my cousins Margaret, Amelia, Andrew and Michael Gardiner. They have been promised sweets for good behaviour, and so far they have been golden."

"Ah, sweets are wonderful," said Matthew with a friendly smile. "When you have finished browsing through the store, we have a selection in this case over here." He motioned to a long glass enclosed case filled with a variety of candies. "Charlotte is just in the back helping me with an order of lace. I cannot say I have fully learned how to organize them yet. I will let her know you are here, Miss Elizabeth." He bowed and stepped through a curtain to the back office of the store.

"Matthew will inherit the store," said Elizabeth in explanation to her companions. "He is learning to run it and does an admirable job. You will not find a more welcoming establishment in all of Meryton—of course, I am a bit partial."

"He seems like a fine young gentleman," said Darcy. "The sort that will be successful."

"Oh, he is determined, I will give you that," said Elizabeth. "He nearly took away my tree climbing and rock throwing titles a few years back."

"And he is the only one of my brothers who does not bear a scar from Elizabeth," said Charlotte approaching the group.

"Impressive," said Darcy.

Elizabeth blushed profusely.

"He is smarter than Jacob and Elijah," said Charlotte. "From an early age, he has always thought things through and weighed the consequences. If only the other two had done so, the surgeon would not have had to stitch them up so often."

~*~*~*~*~*~

The party from Longbourn took their time making the rounds of the store. The little boys found a section of toys to entertain them while the girls looked over the lace that Charlotte brought out from the store room. Darcy quietly slipped to the counter and struck up a hushed conversation with Matthew. "So, you can send all of these items to Netherfield by Christmas Eve?"

"Certainly, sir." Matthew noted the instructions on the receipt. "May I help you with anything else, Mr. Darcy?"

"Yes, when the children select their candies, could you put an extra aside to accompany this order?"

"It would be my pleasure."

"Thank you. Sweets selection is next, is it not Michael?" Darcy looked down at the youngster who had appeared at his side. "Can you go get the others?" Michael nodded his head and raced off to get his brother and sisters. When the candy selection had been completed and each child had their treat, Elizabeth collected the bag of sweets and promptly told them that they could eat them in the carriage.

Matthew slipped the totalled bill to Darcy discreetly. "I shall pay Mr. Lucas and be out directly," he said to Elizabeth. She smiled and moved the group towards the door where they waited for him.

"That Mr. Darcy is a fine gentleman, Charlotte," said Matthew as he watched the group leave the store. "Gave me an order to fill for the Gardiner children. Will you help me gather the items? I need to have it delivered to Netherfield before Christmas Eve."

"Give me the list," said Charlotte holding out her hand.

"You know," said Matthew as he gave her the receipt, "his cousin, the Colonel, is not a bad fellow either." He winked at her and laughed as she blushed.

~*~*~*~*~

Elizabeth took particular care on Christmas Eve to prepare for dinner. The visitors from Netherfield were to dine with her family and then attend services with them. It would be the first time that she would be officially in public on the arm of Mr. Darcy.

"You look lovely." Jane wrapped her arms around her sister from behind and propped her chin on Elizabeth's shoulder as they both looked in the mirror. "Stop fiddling with your dress; it is perfect, as is your hair."

"I just want him to feel proud to have me at his side."

"He is," said Jane. "I have seen the look on his face whenever you are on his arm, dearest, and proud only begins to describe it. Completely besotted is more accurate."

"Thank you, Jane."

"Shall we go down and wait for our guests to arrive?"

"In a moment." Elizabeth sat on the bed and patted it in an invitation for Jane to join her. "Are you as excited as I?"

"I believe I am, but I never have been as good at displaying my delight as you."

"I would like to have a measure of your calmness at present," said Elizabeth. "I do feel as if I am about to have one of Mama's fits of nerves." The girls laughed. "She has not needed her salts since we returned, have you noticed, Jane?"

"There seems to be many changes which have

taken place at Longbourn in our absence," said Jane. "Mary is no longer a mouse, Kitty has refused to follow Lydia on more than one occasion and Lydia's behaviour, while not reserved, has certainly begun to come under regulation."

"Papa is not spending as much time in his library, either," said Elizabeth. "Did he tell you that Lydia and Kitty are no longer completely out to society?"

"Yes, and I have heard Lydia whine about how she would so dearly like to see the officers again, but Papa absolutely refuses to allow it."

"It is because she put us in danger with Mr. Wickham," said Elizabeth. "Father will allow her to be at social gatherings, but she may only socialize with those he allows. Not even Mama is allowed to grant permission. I can understand how she must be feeling the sting of such strictures. They are new to her."

"But, they are of her own doing," said Jane firmly.

"I hear a carriage," Elizabeth jumped from the bed and walked quickly to the window. "There are three carriages to be precise—Mr. Bingley's, Viscount Bladen's and Lord Matlock's. We must go down," Elizabeth grabbed her sister by the hand and pulled her from the room.

The sitting room filled quickly once the carriages had been divested of their occupants.

"Mrs. Gardiner," said Darcy, "I have a few surprises for the children. Would you like to hide them until the morning, or would it be acceptable to give them to them now?" His excitement was clearly written across his face.

"I do not see how I can refuse you the right to witness their delight," said Mrs. Gardiner. "The children are still above stairs in the nursery. Shall we take their surprises to them there?"

"A delightful idea."

Mrs. Gardiner pulled Elizabeth close and whispered, "I thought I told you to not let him spoil the children."

"I had no idea, Aunt. It appears he can be covert when he wishes."

"My children will miss you both sorely when you have left town for Pemberley."

"Then you shall have to visit," said Elizabeth.

A squeal of delight greeted them as Mr. Darcy entered the nursery with arms full of gifts. There was a new soldier for Andrew, a boat for Michael, gloves of creamy white for Amelia and a small brown reticule decorated with golden embroidered flowers for Margaret. There was also a favourite sweet that was not to be eaten until after dinner.

"Mr. Darcy, I am most impressed by your selections. It appears you have discovered all of my children's favourites."

"It is not a difficult task when one listens and observes," said Darcy trying to deflect the praise.

"Ah, but not all actually listen to children, you know," said Mrs. Gardiner. "It is an admirable trait to be sure."

"I find your children have very good taste when choosing favourites," said Darcy taking Elizabeth's hand and placing it in the crook of his arm.

"Indeed they do," said Mrs. Gardiner with a laugh. "Shall we return to the adults?"

"I was hoping to have a few moments alone with Miss Elizabeth as I also have a gift for her."

"May I suggest the back parlour," said Mrs. Gardiner. "It may be free or nearly free of people. That should allow for some privacy."

"Would you show him the way, Aunt? I have a gift for Mr. Darcy as well, but I must stop in my room to retrieve it."

"Certainly. If you will follow me, Mr. Darcy."

Not more than five minutes later, the couple was seated in a corner of the back parlour while Jane and Mr. Bingley were seated in the opposite corner.

Elizabeth chewed on her bottom lip and held out her gift to Mr. Darcy. "I hope you like it. Georgiana assured me you would, but we were about to arrive late at your aunt's house so she may have just been trying to hurry me along." Elizabeth babbled on as her nerves got the better of her.

"I would treasure anything you gave me," said Darcy, "simply because it meant you were thinking of me."

"Georgiana said something very similar," Elizabeth said with a laugh. "Perhaps I should have taken her suggestion and wrapped up a rock."

"A rock?"

"As I said, she was trying to hurry me along and suggested I was spending far too much time being indecisive."

"I cannot imagine you being indecisive."

"I have never bought a gift for a gentleman before except for my uncle and father, and well, the man I was thinking of was dearer to me than even them. I wanted it to be a gift that spoke to who he was." Elizabeth dropped her eyes to study her hands. "Please open it. My nerves cannot handle the suspense much longer."

"This is very fine quality," said Darcy as he ran his hand over the cravat. "And what does this say about the man?"

"It says he is of very fine quality—the best of men," said Elizabeth, a faint pink blush gracing her cheeks.

"Thank you," said Darcy softly. Her admission causing his admiration for her to swell within his chest. He felt the second package. "This feels like a book," he said as he untied the ribbon. "Ah, I guessed correctly." He turned the book over in his hands. "Oh, it is one of my favourite poets, but it is scuffed? Dare I ask to what this speaks?"

"It seems that throwing books can cause damage to their lovely covers," said Elizabeth.

"You threw this?" Darcy's eyebrows knit in confusion.

"Remember the package I went to retrieve when..." She rubbed her arm. "I threw it at his gun. It helped me save Andrew."

"You bought this on that day?" He ran his fingers gently over the scar on the cover.

"Yes. I thought of returning and buying one that was not damaged, but decided that the scuffed one spoke more than a perfectly unmarred copy would. The contents of the book speak to the emotions of the man—hidden behind an unassuming exterior much like the simple brown cover of this book. The scuff speaks not only of his struggle to protect those he loves, but it also speaks to the willingness I have to fight to be part of his life."

Darcy turned the book over in his hands studying it. "My love, I have never received a more thoughtful gift. I shall treasure it always just as I treasure you." He placed the book on a small table. "My gift to you symbolizes just how precious you are to me. Although the gift is of great price, its price is a pittance next to the value of the woman who wears it." Darcy drew a small box out of his pocket and removed a necklace from it. It was a golden chain with a pendant made from a perfect pearl. "Perfect pearls are rare to find. There is great danger to the diver, yet he descends into the ocean to secure his treasure. Many divers spend the whole of their lives seeking to find such a pearl.

Indeed, some lose their lives in the quest. So it is for me. My life is lost to your love. You are a treasure of great value, Elizabeth. I will spend my whole life seeking to be worthy of you. Your love is beyond price."

Elizabeth placed her hand lightly on his cheek. "I have never felt so precious. Thank you, Fitzwilliam." She leaned forward and kissed him.

He unclasped the chain and reaching forward, encircled her neck and clasped it again. He pulled back ever so slightly, his hands still resting at the back of her neck and looked at the necklace, the pearl resting just below the hollow at the base of her throat. "Lovely," he breathed as he drew her head towards his for a second brief kiss—much shorter in duration than either of them wanted.

"Ah, here they are Thad," said Richard entering the parlour. "Seems we may be intruding." He shot a wicked smile at his cousin.

"We were just exchanging gifts," shot back Darcy.

"So Mrs. Gardiner told us," said Richard. "Sent us to tell you that dinner is almost ready."

"And to keep an eye on us?" said Elizabeth arching an eyebrow.

"I suppose there was a bit of that, too," he admitted. His eyes twinkled. "We did take our time finding the room, though."

"Yes, your housekeeper was gracious enough to re-route us twice," said Thad. "She is not quite sure how anyone could get lost in a house of this size—especially a colonel in His Majesty's army. Even Richard did not wish to push his luck with a third deliberate wrong turn."

"So, Bingley, was he well behaved?" asked Richard.

"Oh, is there someone in the room besides Miss Bennet?" responded Bingley with a devilish grin.

"Well, I can tell you they were both well-behaved," said Jane. "Although Mr. Bingley may not be able to pay attention to more than one thing at a time, I can assure you I am capable."

"I am hurt. I thought I had your undivided attention," said Bingley playfully. "Actually, we both were enjoying the performance. Darcy here can be quite the romantic."

Darcy glowered at his friend.

"Yes." Jane placed a hand on her heart and sighed. "It was quite beautiful."

"Perhaps you should have been taking notes, Mr. Bingley?" teased Elizabeth.

Bingley smiled in return and took an imaginary notebook from his pocket. Pretending to write, he muttered, "Scuffed books are treasures." He scratched it out, "No, that was not it. What was it, Darcy, old man?"

"I shall not repeat it," growled Darcy.

"It was perfect." Elizabeth laid her hand on his and gave him a loving smile. "Now, for dinner." She rose, and Jane came to take her arm.

"You gentlemen will be joining us, will you not?" Jane called over her shoulder. Bingley stared at her, his mouth agape.

"Forgot that Jane is often Elizabeth's second, Bingley, old man?" asked Darcy. "Poke one and earn the disapprobation of two."

Chapter 13

"That is a pleasant sight," commented Anne as she dealt the last of the cards.

"What is a pleasant sight?" asked Elizabeth.

"Darcy and Thad actually talking to each other." Anne nodded her head toward the group of gentlemen conversing on the opposite side of Netherfield's drawing room.

"Do they not normally talk to each other?" Elizabeth arranged her cards in her hand.

"Oh, Darcy usually tries to converse with Thaddeus, but his efforts are met with short replies which frequently spark debate," said Anne. "But, I have not heard one word of argument since we arrived. And it has been four days!"

Mary laid a trump card on the pile taking the trick. "Mr. Darcy is no longer the competition."

Four pairs of eyes turned towards her.

"What do you mean?" asked Anne.

"Mr. Darcy has made it clear, has he not, that he is not going to marry you?" Mary questioned. Anne nodded her head. "Then, the jealousy which fueled the arguments is gone."

"Do you think Thaddeus was jealous of Darcy?" asked Anne.

"Indeed, I do," said Mary. "I have only known you and Lord Bladen for a few days, but it is easy to see he is as smitten with you as you are with him. With just the right amount of encouragement, I do believe we could be having five weddings in the very near future."

"Five?" gasped Charlotte closing her book and focusing her entire attention on the game and the conversation at the table.

Mary lay her cards face down on the table and used her fingers to count off the couples. "Mr. Collins and myself, Mr. Bingley and Jane, Mr. Darcy and Lizzy, Lord Bladen and Miss deBourgh, and Colonel Fitzwilliam and you. That is five weddings all told." Mary laughed softly at the shocked look on Charlotte's face. "You are not going to deny there is something between you and the colonel, now are you, Charlotte?"

"No," said Elizabeth. "I do not think she could—not considering how we have all witnessed their looks and smiles as well as the flushed cheeks whenever they are in company." A twitter of laughter passed around the group.

Mary gathered her hand and tapped it on the table. "Back to matters at hand," she said as if she were conducting a business transaction. "If two of those weddings are to happen at all, you, Miss deBourgh, must work on Lord Bladen."

"Me?" Anne's eyebrows shot up in surprise.

Mary proceeded to relate to Anne the details of her mother's visits to both Elizabeth and herself.

"My goodness," gasped Anne. "I knew my mother was not well-pleased and in quite a fit of temper, but to be so...so...so hateful?"

"Mary has a plan," said Elizabeth, "and your uncle, my uncle, my father and I have agreed to it. However, it would be much easier to accomplish with your help, Miss deBourgh."

"Please, if we are to be co-conspirators may we not dispense with the formalities and use our Christian names?" Anne placed her cards on the table and shifted her full attention to Mary. "Mary, please tell me what I am to do."

"Your mother cannot insist upon you marrying Mr. Darcy if you are already married, now can she?" Anne's eyes grew wide while her cheeks grew rosy. Mary continued, "Lord Matlock has begun work to transfer your inheritance of Rosings to your control; thereby, removing it and the authority over the living at Hunsford from your mother. So, all that remains for you to do is marry Lord Bladen."

"Ah, that is why my uncle has requested a meeting," said Anne. "I must admit, I look forward to being the mistress of my own estate." She smiled broadly at the thought. "And, this will mean that the happy establishment of Mr. and Mrs. Collins in the living at Hunsford will become a foregone conclusion with no threat of disquiet."

Mary nodded. "That was my hope."

"As for marrying Thaddeus," Anne continued, "While I grant you it is a most agreeable prospect, I cannot guarantee I will be able to persuade him to act in such a way."

"My dear Anne, a few smiles sent his direction, and I dare say he shall be yours. Even now, his eyes have rarely left you." Jane quietly took yet another trick.

Anne cautiously turned to look at the group of

young gentlemen across the room. Meeting Thad's eyes she smiled. She saw him inhale quickly before he returned her smile, and she demurely dropped her eyes.

"I see what you mean, Jane. I think Mary's plan could prove to be quite amusing."

~*~*~*~*~*~

"Gentlemen," said Lord Matlock who had been watching the interactions of the group of young ladies for some time, "I believe Anne has just been apprised of Miss Mary's plan, and she seems quite pleased with it, if I am reading her expressions aright. It appears I may be gaining a niece and two daughters before long."

"Two daughters?" questioned Sir William.

"It appears Anne holds the affection of my eldest son while my youngest son seems quite smitten with your daughter, Sir William. If you watch, I think his affections are reciprocated."

"I have no need to watch, Lord Matlock. I can assure you I am already aware of where my daughter's affections lie. Am I to understand you would not be opposed to such a match?"

"I would never be opposed to a match forged out of love for either of my sons as long as the woman is sensible, of good moral character, and well-matched to my son's personality. Your daughter is all of those things and more importantly, my wife approves of her." The men shared a hearty laugh at this. "Would I be correct in thinking your daughter would not be the sort of lady who would be disenchanted with the lesser inheritance of a second son? There is a small estate which will be his as soon as he sells out his commission, an action I see him taking soon. The income is not large, but perfectly adequate for a family."

"Money has never been a motivating factor for Charlotte. All she has ever wanted is a comfortable situation where she will not be a burden on her family. In fact, I have often worried she would settle for a marriage of convenience. I am happy to know that both her wishes and mine might be satisfied should your son be persuaded to make a move." Sir William chuckled.

"In truth, I have never seen Richard so reserved. Usually, if there is a desired outcome, he forms a plan and executes it—it is why he was so well-suited to the military." Lord Matlock pushed his chair away from the table and extended his legs crossing them at the ankle. "Perhaps he needs a little push from his father. I would venture he is not just uncertain about the young lady's affection, but also about my reaction to a choice outside the ton. Leave it to me, Sir William. I shall let him know he has nothing to fear from his family."

"You certainly are quite singular, Lord Matlock." Sir William studied the man. "Most men of your rank would not consider allowing such a match."

"Yes, my singularity often astounds my peers and my family, and I quite enjoy it—especially when it guarantees the happiness of those who are closest to me."

"Well," said Mr. Bennet. "I believe it is time for us old folk to make ourselves scarce so the youngsters can work out their happiness. Gardiner, do you not think it is time to get the children home and tucked in?" Mr. Bennet slapped Mr. Gardiner on the back. "I shall offer to send the carriage back for my daughters; although, I believe there will be at least one young man who will object and offer to escort them home." He turned to Sir William. "I am sure you could convince Charlotte to remain and travel home with my girls." Sir William nodded.

"It is getting late for the children," said Mr. Gardiner with a smile. "I shall take the first hit in breaking up the party. It has been an enjoyable evening. Perhaps that poesy ring in a certain young man's pocket will find its home on a certain hand before the night is through."

"There are actually two rings awaiting acceptance, Gardiner. I had a busy schedule of interviews earlier today," said Mr. Bennet. "I hope your wife is prepared to deal with my wife's effusions when the glad tidings are made known."

"I am not sure any of us can be prepared for that," said Mr. Gardiner. "It is fortunate I brought an extra bottle of port with me as our nerves may need it." The gentleman again shared a hearty laugh. Rising, Mr. Gardiner said, "Madeline, I believe it is time to get the children home to bed."

Mr. Bennet followed suit. "Mrs. Bennet, it is time. Mr. Collins, my carriage is at your disposal to return Mary and my two youngest daughters to Longbourn; Mrs. Bennet and I shall travel with the Gardiners. Jane, Elizabeth, I shall send the carriage back for you later. There is no need for you to rush away from your friends."

"Charlotte, Mr. Bennet, has offered to let you

travel home with Lizzy and Jane. Stay and enjoy yourself," said Sir Willliam.

"Mr. Bennet," said Bingley. "There is no need to send your carriage back. I shall make sure the ladies are escorted home."

A smile tugged at Mr. Bennet's mouth, and he gave a covert wink to Lord Matlock. "Mr. Bingley you are all kindness. Your assistance is greatly appreciated, is it not, Mrs. Bennet?"

"Indeed, most appreciated," agreed Mrs. Bennet.

"Glub, glub, glub." Michael raced into the room ahead of a harried Miss Lucy and climbed into Elizabeth's lap waving the gloves in her face.

"Do you wish for help, Michael?" Elizabeth stilled the waving gloves and placed Michael's hands in his lap.

"Help, please," said Michael.

"Much better." Elizabeth took the gloves from the child and helped him put them on.

"Say goodnight to Jane and Lizzy, children," said Mrs. Gardiner.

Michael threw his arms around Lizzy and gave her a kiss. "Night, Lizzy," he said before he slid off her lap and headed to Jane.

"The carriage is waiting, children," said Mr. Gardiner when all the appropriate good nights had been said.

Michael stood in front of Mr. Darcy looking up at him. "May I help you, Master Michael?"

A smile lit the young boys face. "Shoulders, please?"

"You would like to ride to the carriage on my shoulders?"

"Please," said Michael, his head bobbing up and down.

"Very well." Darcy scooped the youngster up and onto his shoulders while the child giggled in delight. "Andrew, shall I see if your steed would be willing to give you a gallop to the carriage?"

Andrew clapped his hands. "Yes, please."

"Richard, are you willing?" asked Darcy.

"Of course," said Richard crouching down so Andrew could climb on his back. He snorted and stomped his foot sending all the children into a fit of giggles. Then he galloped away to the waiting carriage.

~*~*~*~*~*~

Elizabeth pulled her shawl a little tighter around her shoulders and rubbed her injured arm as she watched the carriages pull away from the front of the house.

"Are you well?" asked Darcy. "Is your arm paining you?"

"I am well, Fitzwilliam. My arm is just a little sore from yesterday."

"Yesterday?"

"We have a small Feast of Stephen for the staff at Longbourn each year. The ladies of the house prepare the meal. I think my arm is just sore from the stirring and washing. Nothing a bit of rest and Charlotte's tea will not cure. Do not worry, sir." She laced her arm through his and snuggled closer to him than was entirely proper.

"It is a warm night for December," commented Darcy. "Would you care for a quick turn around the side garden? It is in view of the drawing room."

"I would like that very much, sir. I was getting tired of sitting in the same attitude for so long and since Miss Bingley is not here to escort me about the drawing-room, I shall have to fall on your mercy."

Darcy laughed. "I am glad Miss Bingley is not here, Elizabeth."

"As am I."

They had come to a bend in the path leading past a stand of tall bushes surrounding a sitting area. Darcy pulled Elizabeth off the path and behind the bushes. He wrapped his arms around her and kissed her gently. Stepping back he reached into his pocket and drew something out.

"I spoke to your father."

Delight filled her eyes, but he placed a finger on her lips so he could continue without interruption.

"My love, you hold my heart. Though I faltered in my behaviour and disparaged with my words upon our first meeting, I believe you have held it since then, and it shall never truly be mine again — nor do I ever wish to have it returned." He opened his hand revealing a band of gold engraved on the outside with entwined hearts and flowers. "Elizabeth Bennet, would you do me the honour of standing at the end of a court under a gauge with me and promise to be my wife?"

She placed her hand on top of his open one. She blinked back tears and nodded. "Fitzwilliam Darcy, I love you with every piece of my being and shall continue to do so for as long as I live. I would be honoured to be your wife."

"My father gave this ring to my mother on their

betrothal. It is inscribed. *Love of my heart.*" He placed the ring on her finger and a kiss on her hand before drawing her to him and giving her a long and passionate kiss.

"Are you cold?" he asked when he felt her shiver in his arms.

"No," she said softly, "But I think we should go inside anyway."

"Is something wrong?" asked Darcy in concern.

"Nothing a marriage will not fix, sir." Elizabeth gave his hand a tug, urging him to follow her back to the house. "Might I suggest a short engagement," she threw over her shoulder.

"Oh," was all Darcy said as he followed behind her, a very satisfied look upon his face.

~*~*~*~*~*~

"Did you lose your way when returning to the house, cousin?" asked a smirking Richard.

"No, we decided to take a turn around the garden before returning." Darcy stood in the entry way to the drawing room, Elizabeth at his side.

"Well, would you look at that!" exclaimed Thad. "It seems we have our first victims of the kissing bough. What do you think, Father?"

"So it would seem," chuckled Lord Matlock.

"Lord Matlock, surely you do not approve of such things?" asked Elizabeth in surprise.

"Normally—no, but I feel that tonight may be an exception," he said giving her a wink. "Something tells me it would not be entirely improper."

"That, Richard, sounds like you have just lost the wager." Thad laughed and slapped his brother on the back.

Elizabeth's eyes narrowed. "And what wager would that be, Colonel?"

"We were wagering on who would fall victim to the kissing bough first—Darcy or Bingley." Richard folded his arms across his chest. "Of course, the bet is only won if the lady kisses the gentleman, so I would not count my money just yet, Brother."

Elizabeth arched a brow. "Are you challenging me, Colonel?"

"Oh, no," groaned Mary, Jane, and Charlotte as one.

"I beg you; do not say it is a challenge," pleaded Jane.

"It was not meant as a challenge. I am simply saying a proper lady would not participate in such activities unless they were engaged or married to the gentleman," explained Richard.

"Well, in that case," said Elizabeth, a smile spreading across her face. "Mr. Darcy, it seems Colonel Fitzwilliam has a wager to lose." She placed her hand on Darcy's cheek.

Georgiana squealed, "Mother's ring! Oh, I shall have a sister."

Enjoying the gasps which circled the room, she pulled his head down to give him a very determined kiss.

"Are there any other wagers Elizabeth can help you with, cousins? I find I am rather enjoying this one," said a satisfied Darcy.

"Seems you owe me twice, brother," laughed Thad. "Once for the kiss and another for being engaged before Bingley."

"You bet against me twice?" said an exasperated Elizabeth.

"And I am happy to have lost," said Richard stepping forward to give his congratulations.

Elizabeth pulled him towards her and whispered, "If you are betting on who will have children first, might I remind you that I hate to lose and will gladly do what I have to do to win. Inform me of the details, and the wager is as good as yours, Colonel."

Richard's face reddened. "Of course, Elizabeth. You will be informed of all future wagers," he stammered.

"Cousin Elizabeth," said Mr. Collins. "How can you be engaged to Mr. Darcy when Lady Catherine says he is engaged to her daughter?"

"Dear Mr. Collins," said Elizabeth taking his hands. "Anne has never been engaged to Mr. Darcy."

"But, Miss deBourgh..." Mr. Collins' confusion rendered him near speechless.

"I apologize, Mary. I know I promised I would not interfere, but. . ." Elizabeth looked at her sister for approval.

Mary nodded her consent, so Elizabeth continued. "Mr. Collins, your concern for the emotional well-being of your future patroness does you credit. However, your concern is not necessary since Miss deBourgh's heart has never been engaged where Mr. Darcy is concerned. In fact, her heart has, for some time, been engaged elsewhere." Elizabeth gave a long look toward Lord Bladen until he caught her eye. Then, she raised one eyebrow and smiled at him. "I pray in that case her heart is not rejected." She continued to hold Lord Bladen's gaze for a moment longer before turning again to Mr. Collins. "Miss deBourgh is unharmed by my engagement to Mr. Darcy."

"I believe you have been called out, son," Lord Matlock whispered in Thad's ear. "Miss Lucas, how go the preparations for the Twelfth Night Ball?" he asked trying to turn the conversation.

"They are progressing nicely, my lord," said Charlotte.

"Will it be a crush?" asked Lady Matlock.

"It always is, my lady. There are many who visit from away that add to our usual number."

"Oh," said Jane, "I heard just today that Mr. Cartwell and his brother will be attending,"

"Cartwell has family around here?" asked Mr. Darcy in surprise. Alexander Cartwell was a wealthy and well-respected member of the ton.

"Yes," said Elizabeth, "his sister and her husband have an estate just five miles the other side of Meryton."

"And he frequents Meryton assemblies?" asked Darcy.

"Yes, Mr. Darcy, some people enjoy our assemblies," said Elizabeth with an arched smile which made Bingley and Richard laugh while Darcy coloured.

"And we all know why he has found them so enjoyable of late," said Mary. "Do we not, Charlotte?"

"I am sure I have no idea about what you speak," retorted Charlotte a bit too quickly.

"Come now, Charlotte. You know he has favoured you since your first meeting," said Elizabeth. "It really is too bad you do not favour him as it would be a most advantageous match, my dear." She spoke to Charlotte but looked at Richard.

"And son number two gets called out," muttered an amused Lord Matlock to his glass of brandy. Thad cocked his head and looked at his father.

"You really are a very strange friend, Elizabeth Bennet," said Charlotte. "Do you really wish to speak of missed opportunities for advantageous matches?"

"No, Charlotte, we do not," said Jane grasping Charlotte's arm hard enough that her fingers turned white. "I am sure Lizzy will behave herself."

She shot a look at her sister which brooked no argument.

"Suffice it to say, gentlemen, there will be many a sad fellow when news of the elder Bennet sisters being off the market is published," said Charlotte.

"Indeed?" said Richard, his curiosity aroused. "A tale for another day, Miss Lucas?"

"If you wish, Colonel," said Charlotte.

"Charlotte!" exclaimed Elizabeth in a severe tone, although the self-satisfied smile she gave Richard led him to believe that he had just been deftly maneuvered.

"I really do like her," said Lord Matlock to his wife.

Mrs. Hurst let out a laugh which she had been trying to contain for some time. "Oh, my. Forgive me, but the lamenting in Hertfordshire will be nothing compared to the caterwauling in town." She collapsed in laughter until tears came to her eyes. "Perhaps if Miss Lucas is set against him, we could introduce Mr. Cartwell to our sister, Charles." And she was off again in a fit of laughter.

"Perhaps we should meet the gentleman first and see if he deserves such punishment," suggested Mr. Hurst, which caused a general lapse into laughter.

"I am for bed," said Lady Matlock stifling a yawn. "Henry, you will not be long?"

"I am right behind you, my lady."

"Georgie, you will stay with Anne, will you not? I would hate to abandon her."

"Of course, Aunt. I wanted to play the pianoforte for a while before retiring. Anne, will you join me?"

The Matlocks and Hursts retired to their rooms while Thad escorted Georgiana and Anne to the pianoforte where he took a seat near Anne. The Bennet carriage arrived first and Mr. Collins, Mary, Kitty and Lydia left. The rest of the couples strolled about the garden in the brilliant moonlight. Eventually, each pair found a different path.

"Darcy, Bingley, the carriage is here," called Richard.

"Mr. Bingley and Jane will be along shortly, Colonel," said Elizabeth. "I believe Mr. Bingley needs to settle some business with my sister. Too bad he was not quicker, or you could have won at least part of the bet." Elizabeth laughed. "If they are not here in a few minutes, I shall have to send one of you gentlemen to collect them." She leaned a bit closer to Richard and spoke softly, "I shudder to think what I might have to do to win the next bet for you if we allow them alone for too long."

"You are enjoying tormenting me over my loss, are you not?" growled Richard.

"Indeed, I am. Just retribution for betting against me and forcing me to act in such an unlady-like fashion."

"You did not seem to mind the activity," said Richard dryly.

"No, I suppose I rather enjoyed it, but it still does not make it ladylike, now does it?"

"Darcy, would you please take the lovely Miss Elizabeth into the carriage? I shall hunt down Bingley if he is not here in two minutes," growled Richard.

Elizabeth's eyes twinkled and her mouth wore a smile that was somewhere between impertinent and sympathetic. "I am sorry, Colonel. I will stop tormenting you," she said as she allowed Darcy to hand her into the carriage.

Charlotte shook her head. "She will not stop for long. I learned long ago to not go against that girl unless absolutely forced." Charlotte smoothed the furrow between his eyes. "Stop worrying about that. You have a new worry to think on."

"And what is that?"

"You do realize we are now caught between two kissing couples."

Richard sighed, a small smile pulling at his lips. "Would you be opposed to making it three kissing couples?"

"What a lovely idea, Colonel. Shall we go get Anne and Thad?" Charlotte teased.

"No, that would make it four not three," said Richard pulling her close and kissing her soundly.

"Um, Richard?" Bingley waited for Richard to respond, but when he did not, Bingley gave him a gentle poke. "The carriage is waiting." Having gotten Richard's attention, Bingley opened the carriage door.

"Darcy!" "Elizabeth!" Jane and Bingley called out together.

"Whose idea was it to allow those two to be alone in a dark carriage?" Jane stood with her hands on her hips.

There was a chorus of Richard and Colonel Fitzwilliam in reply to her question.

"Yes, I have already witnessed why he wanted them out of his way," huffed Jane indignantly.

"Now, Jane," said Elizabeth as she smoothed her hair and straightened her dress, "I might ask you what you were doing off in the dark garden with Bingley for so long?"

"Talking—not kissing and definitely not sitting on his lap!" scolded Jane. "Some people do not throw propriety out the window just because they are engaged!"

"I have done nothing worse than kiss him," said Elizabeth.

"But kissing leads to . . ."

"I am fully aware of where kissing can lead, but I shall not be led there until I am indeed married."

"Provided the engagement is not too long," mumbled Charlotte earning a dark look from both sisters and a chuckle from Richard.

"You may wish us joy," interjected Bingley. "Jane has agreed to make me the happiest of men."

"Congratulations," said Darcy and Richard as the sisters continued to glare at each other.

"Sweetheart, we should get into the carriage now," coaxed Bingley. "Darcy and Elizabeth will behave themselves, will you not?" Bingley gave

Darcy an imploring look. Conflict always made him uneasy, especially conflict between sisters. He had seen enough female battles when growing up to know to steer clear of upsetting an already out-of-sorts female.

"Of course," said Darcy.

Elizabeth nodded before muttering, "For now."

"Yes, sir," said Richard cheerily, "my money is definitely on you next time, Elizabeth."

"As it should be," retorted Elizabeth before they both burst into laughter.

"Do I want to know of what you two are speaking?" asked Darcy.

"Probably not," said Elizabeth.

"No, but I will tell you later," said Richard.

~*~*~*~*~*~

Bingley and Darcy climbed back into the carriage after bidding goodnight to their ladies.

"Now," said Darcy. "Tell me, of what were you and Elizabeth speaking?"

"Are you sure you wish to know?" asked Richard. "It is a bit scandalous."

Darcy's eyes narrowed, and he folded his arms across his chest. "I wish to know."

"Our comments were in reference to wagering about children."

"Children?" asked Bingley. "Whose children?"

Darcy pinched the bridge of his nose and shook his head. "I am guessing ours, Bingley."

"Precisely," said Richard.

"But we do not have children," said Bingley.

"It is about who will produce an heir first. Am I right, Richard?" asked Darcy. Richard nodded.

"Produce an—what?" Bingley sat bolt upright on his bench, and Richard could feel his glare penetrating the darkness. "Who speaks of such things with ladies? For that matter, who bets on such things?"

"The same people who bet on engagements and kisses, Bingley," said Darcy dryly.

"There is no bet. It was all in jest, and I was not the one to bring it up. Elizabeth did. She seemed rather put out by our other bets and that I had not placed my money on her." Richard laughed. "She told me if I dared to bet on who would have the first child, I am to inform her, and she will—and I quote—'gladly do whatever I have to do to win.'"

"I thought ladies shied away from such things," said Bingley. "I have always heard that such, um, activities were the cause of fear for most young brides."

"Shy and fearful are not exactly words I would use to describe Elizabeth," said Darcy.

"No, considering what we saw upon opening the door tonight," scoffed Bingley. "You do not suppose she is actually wanton?"

"Bingley!" Darcy growled.

Richard put a hand on his cousin's chest, staying him from lurching across the carriage at his friend.

"In my experience, gentlemen, wanton women do not beat up young men and leave them bound and bleeding in cloakrooms because they make inappropriate advances," said Richard.

"She did that?" asked Bingley in astonishment.

"Technically she did the beating, and Jane did the tying," said Richard.

"Oh," said a stunned Bingley.

"Now women who are violently in love with the man they are to marry and are of the—shall we say—less retiring variety have been known to be, um," Richard searched for the right word. "enthusiastic."

"To her credit, gentlemen, the carriage was not

her fault," said Darcy. "In fact, she has never been the instigator—except when causing Richard to lose his bet."

"Tsk, Tsk, cousin," Richard chided in a teasing tone. "Shall I inform my mother of your behaviour?"

"I sincerely doubt it would be of much use. She is the one who left us alone the first time—at your father's request."

"My mother?"

"Yes, your mother, Richard. And I think you can forget about telling Georgie either since she left us together the second time and blocked the door to keep your mother from entering." There was a smugness to Darcy's voice.

"Darcy, you are incorrigible! Where is the man who was too frightened to make coherent speech in her presence, who was the pillar of propriety?" asked Richard.

"Gone," said Darcy. "The fear of losing her first to a gunman and then to the scheming of our aunt has totally driven him away."

"He has done it again, Bingley. He has given such a sensible answer that makes it impossible for us to tease him."

"Oh, I think there is still one thing he fears, Richard."

"And pray tell, what is that, Bingley?"

"A long engagement."

Darcy groaned as the others laughed.

Chapter 14

Darcy surveyed the assembly hall. Aside from the decorations of the season, it looked very much the same as it did when he had first entered it with Bingley. Then he was a stranger, a spectacle at which to gawk, a wealthy gentleman in want of a wife. Much had happened between that day, a fortnight after Michaelmas, and Twelfth Night. He was no longer a stranger, and he had no want of a wife, or at least soon he would not. The assembly hall was still crowded with noisy people enjoying themselves, but this time, Darcy was one of them. Elizabeth stood beside him with her hand resting on his arm. He covered her hand with his and gave it a squeeze.

"Mr. Darcy, are you well?" asked a startled Elizabeth.

"I have never been better, my love. And I do not

think I have ever enjoyed an assembly as much as this one," he said as he smiled down at her.

"Miss Elizabeth, I hear I am to wish you joy," said a fine looking young man escorted by a lovely young lady.

"Thank you, Mr. Marsden. May I present my betrothed, Mr. Darcy of Pemberley in Derbyshire. Mr. Darcy, this is Mr. Marsden of Fairview in Hertfordshire and Miss Weston."

"Marsden?" repeated Darcy.

"I see you have heard of me, Mr. Darcy." He smiled sheepishly. "To this day, I shy away from cloakrooms."

"I believe I owe you a debt of gratitude, sir." Darcy extended his hand and gave Mr. Marsden's a firm shake. "It seems your, uh, lesson in self-defense proved useful in apprehending a scoundrel."

"Ah, yes, I had heard about that. The arm is all healed, Miss Elizabeth?"

Elizabeth coloured slightly. "Yes, thank you. A bit of a scar, but nothing worse."

"I should warn you. I happened to overhear your father sending any who wish to dance with your younger sisters to you for approval. A few have already slunk off." He bowed and said, "Again, joy to you, Miss Elizabeth and good luck, Mr. Darcy."

"Now you know why I was one of those ladies sitting on the sidelines at your first Meryton assembly. Fear kept me there—not mine, but theirs." Elizabeth laughed.

"Some of us bear the scars which remind us why we should remain fearful, Miss Elizabeth," said another young gentleman, who rubbed a hand across a white scar just at his hairline in front of his left ear.

"One should not sneak up on another and threaten to run them through and not expect to be injured," said Elizabeth.

"Yes, our band of pirates never could capture your ship, now could we?"

"Indeed, you could not. I had the best sword-wielding deck hands in all of Hertfordshire. It is a good thing our swords were only made of sticks, is it not?" said Elizabeth.

"Had they been made of anything stronger, I shudder to think of what might have happened to me when you spun around and knocked me on the head."

Elizabeth turned to Darcy who was listening in amusement. "Mr. Darcy, this former pirate is Mr. Joshua Lucas, Charlotte's eldest brother. Joshua, this is Mr. Darcy of Pemberley in Derbyshire."

Joshua bowed to Mr. Darcy. "It is a pleasure to meet you, sir. Miss Elizabeth's father has sent me over here to gain approval to ask Miss Kitty for a dance." He turned to Elizabeth and added, "I can assure you I will be a perfect gentleman." He looked around her. "However, it appears you are without your sword tonight, so I should be safe."

"Aye, but it could be stashed in the cloakroom with my wrap," teased Elizabeth. "You, of course, have my blessing, Joshua. Go enjoy yourself, but know that I will be watching unless otherwise distracted."

"Perhaps I could be of assistance, Mr. Lucas. I feel as if I may wish to dance, Miss Elizabeth," he said with a wink to Joshua. The young man nodded his appreciation and hurried off to find Kitty.

"I would be delighted to stand up with you, Mr. Darcy, but first..." She turned to speak to a frightened looking young gentleman who had approached her. "Mr. Crenshaw, am I to assume you would also like to dance with one of my sisters?

Miss Lydia, perhaps?"The gentleman in front of her nodded his head. "You are free to ask her," said Elizabeth. "Your brother has told you what happens to those who do not treat others well?"Again the gentleman nodded his head vigorously.

"Good, remember it," cautioned Elizabeth.

"I think he was petrified," said Darcy.

"After what I did to his brother, he should be."

"And what did you do to his brother?"

"He was tormenting a servant girl. He had stolen her basket and was holding it out of her reach, delaying her and putting her in peril of facing who knows what discipline if she lost the basket or was late in returning home. I got the basket back."

"How exactly, did you get the basket back?"

"Did you know that if you strike a person just here," Elizabeth placed a hand on her stomach. "He will double over in pain and anything he has been holding over your head is suddenly within reach? In fact, his hold on it and ability to speak diminishes substantially as well. But you must be careful not to hit too high or too hard as it could do severe damage."

"I am beginning to understand why Mr. Marsden wished me luck," teased Darcy as he took her hand to lead her towards the dance floor.

"After this dance, I believe I may need to have a short discussion with my father. Sometimes his sense of humor goes beyond what it should. You will soon be wondering what kind of harridan you are marrying."

"I already know," said Darcy with a twinkle in his eye. "One who has the good sense to like me, and one who has captured my heart." He lifted her hand and gave it a kiss. "And, Elizabeth, you are not a harridan. You are a protector with an over-developed competitive spirit, which, should Richard and Thad actually make that bet, I will only encourage."

"Mr. Darcy!" said Elizabeth in mock astonishment. "You surprise me, sir." She laughed as she took her stand opposite him in the line.

~*~*~*~*~*~

"Oh, what an enjoyable assembly, is it not, Darcy?" Bingley placed his plate on the table and sat next to his friend.

"Indeed it is," said Darcy. "And you, Richard, are you enjoying the assembly?"

"I am. A beautiful lady at my side and good

friends with which to share my good fortune make just about any event enjoyable." He leaned back contentedly in his chair.

"Before the ladies return," said Thad. "Richard and I had a long talk with Father today. He knows of Richard's selling out, and he approves of both Charlotte and Anne as future daughters."

"And Sir William is pleased with the idea as well. The only hold outs to our happiness are our ladies as we have not yet spoken to them, and, of course, our Aunt." Richard rolled his eyes. "Charlotte is returning to London with us in the morning. Mother has invited her to attend Lady Matlock's Annual New Year Soiree."

"I cannot believe Mr. Collins is dancing at an assembly on his wedding night," said Darcy shaking his head as he watched the newlyweds gathering their supper plates. "I am glad to see them married, though. You know Elizabeth was going to call off our courtship to appease Lady Catherine just so her sister could get married?"

"No," said three male voices. Darcy just nodded his head and sipped his lemonade.

"So the fear of losing her has diminished, cousin?" asked Richard.

"Indeed it has. Although it will not completely go away until we have said our vows and been pronounced man and wife."

Richard clapped Darcy on the shoulder. "Darcy, you have experienced enough loss in your life, you deserve this happiness. Do not allow worry about the what if's take that happiness from you."

"I shall try not to let it, but I may need some help not sinking into worry."

"Count on us, Darcy," said Bingley. "Just say the word and we will be there for you, just as you always have been for us."

"Thank you, Bingley," said Darcy. "Ah, here comes our happiness, gentlemen." A smile suffused his face as they rose to greet the returning ladies.

"It just seems strange," said Elizabeth to Charlotte as they approached the table.

"What seems strange?" asked Richard.

"You really might be too curious for your own good," said Elizabeth.

"Elizabeth was just saying she cannot understand why Mr. and Mrs. Collins are spending their wedding night dancing at an assembly," said Charlotte.

A ripple of laughter went around the group of men.

"I do not see how that is funny." Elizabeth smoothed her skirt as she sat down.

"Oh, but it is as Darcy made the same comment not five minutes ago," said Bingley.

"So how long is it until the wedding?" asked Thad as he assisted Anne in taking a seat.

"One week, four days and ten hours," said Elizabeth. She narrowed her eyes and glared at Charlotte, who had barely caught her laughter. "In one week, four days, and ten hours I shall not have to listen to my mother go on and on about endless tiring details."

"Yes, I am sure that is all that you were thinking about," teased Charlotte.

Elizabeth's face burned with embarrassment. "Charlotte Lucas, just you wait until your turn comes, I will remember this."

"I have no doubt about that. So in for a penny, in for a pound," said Charlotte. "Colonel, did you notice she did not deny what I said?"

"Quite right, Miss Lucas. Now, what else could she have been thinking about?"

"You are both horrid!" Elizabeth rose quickly from her chair startling those who sat with her. "I need to walk," she stated before stalking off, trailed by Darcy.

"Oh, dear." Jane twisted her napkin. "Mother really has been a trial, although that has not been the only source of frustration." A chuckle went around the group. Jane blushed. "Yes, that...and she is quite worried about how she will be received in London. As you know, there are two ladies in particular who may have spent the last two and a half weeks poisoning the pool, so to speak."

"I had not thought of that." Charlotte drummed her fingers on the table, her face full of concern. "She will not do anything as foolish as trying to abandon ship if she thinks the waters have been too poisoned and pose a threat to Mr. Darcy? Do you?"

"You know as well as I, she will put everyone's well-being ahead of her own," said Jane.

"Then we must convince her that more harm would come to Darcy from her defection than by any poisoned social waters," said Richard. "His greatest fear at present is losing her. I honestly do not think he would recover."

Bingley nodded. "Yes, he said as much right before you returned to the table."

"Perhaps we worry needlessly," said Thad. "Perhaps, Darcy will not let that happen. Look at the way he chased after her just now. Have you forgotten his protective side or his determination once his mind is set? I say have faith in him. He would move heaven and earth for her, and you know it."

"Quite right, brother. But, we shall still keep an eye on them. Miss Lucas, would you care for a walk? I think I saw them head down the west corridor."

~*~*~*~*~*~

"Elizabeth, my love, what is wrong?" Darcy reached out and caught her by the elbow. "It is more than your mother. You could still accept teasing when she was upset with you about Mr. Collins. Please tell me. I want...no...I need to help you. You are my world, Elizabeth. If you hurt, I hurt," said Darcy turning her towards him.

"That is just it," said Elizabeth. "I am afraid I will hurt you."

"Exactly how do you imagine you will hurt me?" Darcy drew a breath and braced himself for her reply.

"Your aunt and Miss Bingley have had more than two weeks to spread all sorts of stories about me. Your standing among your peers could be damaged because of your association with me." Elizabeth's bottom lip quivered, and she turned away.

"Elizabeth." Darcy's voice held a warning. "You will not walk away from me because of what some group of people think or do not think of me. I do not care about them or their opinions. I could gladly live my life without ever socializing with them again, but I cannot and will not live my life without you. The only way you could hurt me is by leaving. I need you, Elizabeth. I love you. Please tell me you will not leave me." Darcy grabbed her by the shoulders and turned her to face him.

"But Georgiana's coming out . . ." said Elizabeth softly.

"There are places other than the ton to find a husband. In fact, I am beginning to believe other places are preferable." He smiled softly at her. "I know I found the best woman in the world at a country assembly." He placed a finger under her chin and tilted her face so he could look into her eyes. "You will find even your determined spirit is no match for me when I have set my mind to something as important as this."

Elizabeth looked deeply into his eyes and read the truth of his statements there. Though her eyes glistened and her lips trembled, she attempted to give him an arched smile. "Well, then, sir, it is a good thing I favour your position on this so we will not need to test who is more determined." The tears could be contained no longer. "I love you," she whispered.

Darcy drew her into his embrace. "I will never let you go. Remember that." His voice quavered with emotion as he spoke softly to the top of her head. After a few minutes of standing locked in each other's embrace, Darcy pulled away. "We must get back. One week, four days, and nine and a half hours and then forever," he said as he bent to give her a quick kiss.

Someone cleared their throat behind them. Darcy and Elizabeth jumped, startled that they were not alone.

"Is everything well?" asked Richard.

Charlotte ran to Elizabeth and embraced her. "I am sorry, Lizzy. I had no idea how troubled you were. I promise not to tease you anymore."

Elizabeth laughed. "That, my dear friend, is not a promise you can keep, nor is it one I would wish for you to keep. I should thank you. This conversation," she motioned to Darcy, "had to happen. Without your motivation, it would not have happened so soon, and I would still be troubled."

"So you are no longer troubled?" asked Charlotte.

"Oh, no, I am still troubled unless someone has caused my mother to become a mute and has invented a means to make time go faster, but I am not as troubled." Elizabeth smiled and took Darcy's arm. "Now, Richard, how long until I have an opportunity to tease Charlotte about bridal nerves?" She arched a brow in question. "My money is on you," she said as a parting shot.

Darcy guffawed and slapped his cousin on the back. "And you know how much she hates to lose."

~*~*~*~*~

The morning had dawned crisp and clear. A thin blanket of snow made the sun's rays double in their intensity. Elizabeth yawned and stretched.

She had slept later than usual but not as late as was customary after a night of dancing. Her body cried out for the comfort of her bed as she threw back the covers and rose to prepare for the day—a day that promised plenty of time for rest on the trip to London.

After dressing and having Sarah attend to her hair, she went down to breakfast. Gathering a roll and ham from the sideboard along with a cup of coffee, she sat down and rolled her head to the side to ease a particularly stiff muscle before beginning her repast.

"Tired, dear?" asked Mrs. Gardiner.

"I admit I am, Aunt. I am sure that nothing but the excitement of today's travels could have pulled me from my bed, but there shall be time enough to rest on our journey."

"I hope my children rest." Mrs. Gardiner sighed. "You know how they can get when confined to the carriage."

"Perhaps we can pass them between carriages," suggested Elizabeth with a laugh.

Mrs. Gardiner joined in the laughter. "We would not want to scare off your young man."

"Mrs. Gardiner, I do not think we could scare

him off if we tried." Mr. Bennet put down the paper he had been reading to refill his cup of coffee. "Not even the former victims of Elizabeth's form of justice could shake him last night." Her father's eyes twinkled. Elizabeth opened her mouth to say something, but her father put up his hand to forestall her.

"It appears the gentleman has enough mettle to handle our Lizzy. And as for the children, Mrs. Gardiner, they seem quite taken with Mr. Darcy, and he with them. For someone who appeared so foreboding at first, he really is quite open and gentle with them. You, my dearest Lizzy, have chosen your husband and the father of your children quite well." He gave her a smile, his eyes just a little misty as he once again returned to his paper.

Lizzy rose and walked around the table. Throwing her arms around his neck, she said, "Thank you, Papa. I hope he is as good and loving a father as you."

"And, I hope he is better," said Mr. Bennet. "Now run along and help your aunt get those children ready to go. I should like to enjoy some peace before your mother appears."

Lizzy kissed his cheek. "Yes, Papa."

Chapter 15

One week after returning to town with her aunt and uncle, Elizabeth paced the floor stopping occasionally to peer out of the parlour window.

"How much longer shall our rug have to suffer such abuse?" Mr Gardiner kissed his wife's cheek as he entered the room.

"Not long, my dear. You were fortunate enough to be at work so you have been spared the worst of it." Mrs Gardiner chuckled. "It is at times like these that I am reassured that she is indeed Fanny Bennet's daughter."

Lizzy started at the statement and immediately sat in a chair near the window, her fingers drumming a pattern on the arm.

"It is no good, Lizzy," said her aunt. "You must expend your nervous energy in movement. You will notice you are not the only lady who is uneasy." She nodded toward Jane. "One would think that with such fervent attention, the results would be much better."

Jane smiled. "I have done a rather ill job, have I not? I will likely have to remove all my stitches later and begin again."

"Remember, girls," said their uncle. "Your young men care for you, and your host and hostess for the evening hold you both in high regard. All will be well."

"I shall try to believe you, Uncle." Elizabeth peered out the window and watched an elegant crested coach pull up in front of the house. She sucked in a deep breath and expelled it slowly. Her fingers stopped drumming, and she rose to her feet, an air of calm settling over her. "Come, Jane, our carriage has arrived."

Mr. Gardiner chuckled. "It is truly amazing to see you transform before my eyes, Lizzy." He offered an arm to each niece. "Allow me to escort you two beautiful young ladies to your awaiting conveyance."

~*~*~*~*~*~

A short time later the Darcy coach pulled up in front of Matlock House. Georgiana, Jane, and Elizabeth carefully exited with the help of a footman. Lizzy smiled and murmured her thanks quietly so that no others would hear her address the staff. She was rewarded with a slight nod from the footman. The three ladies linked arms and approached the house.

Just inside the entry another footman waited to receive the ladies' outerwear. Elizabeth again smiled and attempted to make her appreciation known. Again, she was rewarded with a small nod.

Lord Matlock observed her and smiled to himself. "She shall have all my staff charmed before the evening is over," he said to his nephew. "It is the marking of a truly great lady. I have seen many ladies who aspire to greatness, but only those who recognize people from all walks of life truly achieve it. You, my lad, have chosen a diamond of the first waters."

"Thank you, Uncle, but now I would like to greet my jewel."

"Of course, my boy, go take your place at her side." His uncle clapped him on the shoulder. "I shall take my place at your aunt's side before she gives me a scolding for avoiding our guests. They shall be arriving shortly."

Darcy hurried to greet his sister and Jane. Then, turning to Elizabeth, he took her hand and kissed it. "You are beautiful, my dear." He tucked her hand into the crook of his arm and covered it with his own. "All will be well, Elizabeth," he whispered.

"I am trying desperately to believe that."

"Come, we must greet my aunt and uncle." He led her over to the receiving line.

~*~*~*~*~*~

Inside the ballroom, they joined Richard, Thaddeus, Charlotte, and Anne, who were standing in a corner far from the door.

"It is the perfect spot to observe new arrivals." Richard shifted the curtain and peeked out the window. "Bingley is here."

"And his sisters?" asked Elizabeth anxiously.

"Yes, both and Mr. Hurst," Richard replied.

"Do you suppose there will be any wealthy, eligible gentlemen here tonight to whom we might introduce her?"

Thad laughed. "I shall inform you of all shrew-worthy eligible men who enter. We shall take turns introducing them to her."

"They do not have to be shrew-worthy...just

available. The goal is to keep her busy and hopefully happy enough to leave me alone."

"We shall not leave you alone, Elizabeth," said Anne. The others murmured their agreement.

"Let the manoeuvres begin," whispered Richard, a glint of excitement shone in his eyes as the Bingleys and Hursts entered the room.

"He enjoys this far too much," Elizabeth whispered to Darcy. "Perhaps he should consider a post with the foreign office rather than an estate." A laugh rumbled softly in Darcy's chest.

"No need to worry about my cousin. He will find excitement wherever he goes, even if he has to create it."

"Miss Elizabeth." Caroline held out her hands to Elizabeth. "It has been ages since I have seen you. I hope you will enjoy your visit to town. It must be a welcome diversion from the country."

Elizabeth smiled. "Diversions are often welcome. Shall you be leaving the diversions of town behind soon to travel to Netherfield for your brother's wedding? My mother would be delighted to have you in attendance at the breakfast."

Caroline looked at her brother. He had been quite direct with her concerning her behaviour toward Miss Elizabeth. She would, for the present, be residing with the Hursts, and her attendance at his wedding would be decided after seeing her in company this evening. He gave her a small shrug. "My...my... plans are not fully set yet since my brother and sister have just arrived back in town."

"Of course, you will need time to discuss the arrangements. I do hope you will be able to attend."

Jane smiled at Elizabeth. "As do I."

Caroline opened her mouth to reply but was interrupted as a gentleman approached their group with a loud greeting.

"Gentlemen, ladies, it is so good to see you again. Has it been even a week?"

"Only just, Mr. Cartwell. It is a pleasure to see you again as well. Miss Elizabeth was telling me you will be an uncle by the beginning of summer. I trust your sister is well?" Darcy shook Mr. Cartwell's hand.

"She has never looked healthier nor happier. Motherhood seems to agree with her, not all ladies are so fortunate. She requests I extend her gratitude to you Miss Lucas for the tea. She claims it has been invaluable."

"I shall visit her once I return to Hertfordshire next week," said Charlotte.

"Ah, yes, I am to extend her congratulations on your betrothal and inform you she expects a call on your return to hear about the dresses and lace and other wedding preparations." He shook his head as if he could not comprehend the interest in such things.

Bingley stepped forward. "May I introduce my sister, Miss Bingley? Caroline, this is Mr. Cartwell."

"A pleasure," Mr. Cartwell said with a bow as Caroline curtseyed.

"I met him at the Twelfth Night assembly in Meryton," continued Bingley. "His sister's husband owns an estate not far from Netherfield. They are good friends of the Bennets."

"As am I," said Mr. Cartwell. "Mr. Bennet and I have spent many hours hunting and debating." He laughed. "And his brother, Mr. Phillips, is quite the expert in all legal matters pertaining to estates. You would do well to contact him should you decide to stay at Netherfield permanently or just to renegotiate an extended lease. I have had him conduct more than one land deal for me, and I find his work to be excellent."

"I shall keep that in mind," said Bingley.

"If you will excuse me, I see a gentleman to whom I must speak." Mr. Cartwell bowed and strode away.

"Mr. Cartwell frequents Hertfordshire?" asked Caroline.

"Yes, my dear sister, the inhabitants of the country are not all as savage as you believe." Bingley winked at Darcy.

"Indeed there are others of his status who frequent the area," said Charlotte. "We country folk have many connections which would be considered important in town. However, there is little need to flaunt such connections among the residents of Hertfordshire."

"But he is so wealthy and highly respected in the ton." Caroline was trying to reconcile this information within her mind.

"Indeed he is, and he is quite loyal to his friends in Hertfordshire," said Charlotte. "I understand he cut several acquaintances when they made disparaging remarks about his brother, Mr. Hughes. There were those who thought his sister should not marry a country gentleman. He was not well-pleased. I understand those individuals are still working to re-establish their standing within society."

Caroline fidgeted with her fan.

"And now many of Hertfordshire can also count the Earl of Matlock amongst their friends," said Richard.

"As well as his sons, his nephew, and his niece," added Anne.

"They are an agreeable lot in Hertfordshire," said Thad. "I am quite glad to have met them."

"As am I." Darcy smiled at Elizabeth as Richard and Bingley echoed his sentiment.

"It was clever of me to lease an estate in such a lovely part of England, was it not?"

The others, save Caroline, laughed and shook their heads at his exuberance.

The room had become quite full by this time and the musicians were warming up their instruments.

"I see Mother has arrived," whispered Anne. "Uncle Henry had a severe discussion with her about family unity yesterday. I believe she may be too cowed to do much damage tonight."

"I pray you are correct, Anne." Elizabeth

looked at Darcy. "Do we greet her or wait for her to greet us?"

"I prefer never to speak to her again until she apologizes for how she treated you." He squeezed her hand reassuringly.

"Yes, but that does not speak of unity, now does it?"

"Come, children," said Lord Matlock, who had just joined the group during the last few comments. "We shall greet her together before I make my happy announcements."

They approached Lady Catherine and made their greetings. She welcomed Thad and Anne with an open and happy expression but could not contain all of her disdain when greeting Richard and Charlotte and her scowl became more pronounced as she greeted Darcy and Elizabeth.

"Aunt Catherine, it is good to see you this evening." Darcy attempted to use his most engaging voice.

Lady Catherine eyed him carefully. "Is it indeed, nephew?"

"No, but it is the polite thing to say." He gave his aunt a piercing glare.

"Lady Catherine," Elizabeth said with a curtsey.

"Miss Elizabeth." Lady Catherine refused to look at her. "Darcy, I see you are intent on keeping this..." Her voice trailed off as her brother cleared his throat.

Elizabeth squared her shoulders and stood straight. She reached out and grabbed one of Lady Catherine's hands. Lady Catherine tried to snatch it back, but Elizabeth held it firmly. "Lady Catherine, I am sorry you find me to be such a disappointment, and I fear, I must echo your sentiment for I find you to be a disappointment as well."

Lady Catherine's eyes flew to Elizabeth's, and she again attempted to pull back her hand.

"Your nephew and your daughter are happy and yet you insist on pouting and carrying on because you did not get your way. Such behaviour is never tolerated among children because it demonstrates pride which is contrary to the Good Book. How much less should it be accepted in an adult and one who is in such an elevated position that her every word and action instructs those who look up to her?" Elizabeth gave a sad shake of her head. "I am disappointed that neither I nor my children will be able to look up to you as an example to follow while this character flaw remains in your life. However, you are to be my family, and I will love you in spite of it. You will always be welcome at my home as long as you are not pouting." Elizabeth raised Lady Catherine's hand to her lips and placed a kiss on the back of it.

Lady Catherine's eyes were filled with tears. "You...you will love me?" she managed to choke out the words.

"I am quite determined," said Elizabeth. "And I have it on very good authority that I am both obstinate and headstrong, so I can guarantee attempting to dissuade me from it is futile."

A sound similar to a laugh escaped from Lady Catherine. "I shall not make it easy for you."

Elizabeth arched a brow and smiled. "I would not expect anything less. However, if you insist on acting like a child, I will tell you."

Again a sound reminiscent of a laugh escaped from Lady Catherine. She looked at Darcy. "Is she always like this?"

"Usually," he replied.

Lady Catherine turned back to Elizabeth. "I think I could like you. Now, this rudeness of my nephew in greeting his elders, do you think we could do something about that?"

"Hmmm." Elizabeth rubbed her chin as if deep in thought. "That could be a difficult challenge, but with your help, I might be able to bring him up to scratch."

This time a true laugh erupted from the lady, shocking all who stood near.

"Amazing," whispered Thad. "Have you ever heard her laugh, Anne?"

Anne dabbed her eyes with her handkerchief. "Not since I was a child."

For once Darcy did not mind being the object of jest. He beamed proudly at his betrothed.

"I told you, my boy. All the markings of a great lady." Lord Matlock spoke with awe in his voice. "Now, shall we officially announce her as one of the newest members of our family?"

Without waiting for a reply, Lord Matlock walked to the low stage which housed the musicians. He whispered to the conductor and the instruments fell silent. A hush slowly crept across the room.

"Welcome to Matlock House's annual New Year's Ball." Lord Matlock's voice boomed throughout the room. "This year we celebrate not only the new year, but also the new beginning of families branching out from my own. Next week, my nephew, Mr. Fitzwilliam Darcy will wed a truly great lady from Hertfordshire, Miss Elizabeth Bennet. It is with much joy we welcome her into our family."

Applause erupted throughout the room and continued for some minutes until Lord Matlock raised his hand to signal for silence.

"Following shortly after this wedding, my eldest will unite the house of Matlock with the house of deBourgh, and my youngest will marry another treasure from the county of Hertfordshire, Miss Charlotte Lucas." Again there was a hearty round of applause.

"It appears Hertfordshire is a wonderful place to find brides as Mr. Charles Bingley will be joining his friend and my nephew at the altar next week as he marries Miss Elizabeth's sister, Miss Jane Bennet. Customarily, my lovely wife and I lead the first dance of the evening. This year, and hopefully for many years to come, I would ask our four soon-to-be-wed couples to join my wife and me. As always, we invite you to join us. May you all have an enjoyable evening and a prosperous new year."

On cue, the musicians began to play the music

for the first dance, and the four young couples lined up with Lord and Lady Matlock to open the ball. Elizabeth smiled at the man who stood across from her as she took his hand, and for the first time in her life, she thanked the good Lord for her mother's nerves that had caused her to be sent away for her father's peace of mind.

Epilogue

Darcy looked up from the book he had been reading and smiled as his wife entered the library at Darcy House. She had changed from her travelling clothes and was once again wearing the lovely gown she had worn that morning as she stood next to him in the church. He lay his book aside and rose to greet her. "You look refreshed."

"I am, thank you." She walked to where he had been sitting and flipped a few pages of his book. "And you?"

"Quite." Darcy gave a nod of his head to the footman who had escorted Elizabeth to the library. "Kindly inform us when dinner is ready." The man gave a small bow and turned to leave. "We should not be disturbed until then," continued Darcy.

"Of course, sir." The man's features remained composed, but his eyes twinkled with amusement.

Darcy took two steps toward the man and lowered his voice slightly. "As always, your discretion is greatly appreciated." It was both a compliment and a warning.

"As always, sir." A smile threatened to break his solemn mien.

Elizabeth strolled toward the library window. "It was a lovely service, was it not? And the breakfast was delightful."

He came to stand behind her, wrapping his arms around her and drawing her back against his chest. "It may have been. I truly only know that you were lovely, and your presence by my side was delightful."

She sighed and leaned back into him. "Might I ask you a question, Fitzwilliam?"

"You may ask whatever you wish, my love."

"When we first met..." He groaned. "Shall I not ask?" she inquired.

"Please continue. I am only dismayed at the remembrance of my behaviour."

"It was not so bad," she said weakly.

"Yes, my loving wife, it was, but I thank you for attempting to spare my feelings. Now, what did you wish to know? I shall answer whatever you ask." He kissed the side of her neck.

She shivered slightly at the touch. "When you said what you did about me being merely tolerable and not handsome enough to tempt you; were you speaking in haste, in an attempt to quiet your friend?"

"Yes and no."

She turned slightly to look at him inquisitively.

He smiled sheepishly at her. "I did speak in haste but not only to quiet my friend. I wished also to quiet my mind."

"Your mind?" Her eyebrows drew together.

He took a deep breath. "Perhaps I should have said to quiet my desires."

"Oh." She spoke softly and a faint blush crept up her cheeks.

"I do not...or did not...believe in love at first sight. Infatuation at a glance was perfectly rational, but a deep desire to know and be known by another based on the merest of acquaintance seemed improbable, even foolish. Yet, I saw you and all rational thought fled. Within moments of our meeting, I was enchanted by your laugh and smiles; I was bewitched by your eyes. And your figure...well...it was quite tempting. I had not experienced any sensation quite like it. I was convinced it was nothing more than my base desires clouding my perception, playing tricks on my mind—for what else could it be?"

"So you refused to dance with me and spoke an untruth..."

"Because I was afraid. I had been taught from my youth to always keep myself in good regulation, to stand above the crowd, to guard the Darcy name. If I had to think meanly of others to do so, so be it. It is shameful, is it not? To elevate yourself in such a fashion."

"Did you think meanly of me?"

He pulled her closer. "I did. Can you forgive me? I even spoke ill of your family. My behaviour shocked Bingley. I had never been so disagreeable." She stood quietly before him. He waited for her response.

"I also spoke ill of you," she said softly. "I am sorry."

"It is no more than I deserve."

She laughed. "Mary would say not to repay evil with evil but with grace and mercy." She peeked up at him and smiled. "She would be glad to know some of her sermonizing found its way into the mind of one of her listeners." She turned in his embrace. "No, you did not deserve my spiteful words. What you did may not have been right, but my reacting in kind did not mitigate the first offense."

"What I did was not right; I deserved no kindness in return, I can assure you."

She shrugged. "Is that not what grace is? Receiving that which we do not deserve." Her eyes twinkled.

He lifted an eyebrow. "Mary?"

She nodded. "I should really write to her and congratulate her on her success." She reached up and cupped his cheek. "I shall not ask you what you said about my family, for I am well aware of their shortcomings. I will trust since you have attached yourself to my family, you have amended your opinion at least slightly?"

He nodded.

Her thumb stroked his cheek.

"If I am to be honest," he said, "I will have to tell you that I still find your mother and youngest sisters silly. However, after your explanation about your brother, I feel I understand them more fully.

Otherwise, nearly every other impression has been revised."

"Nearly every other impression has been revised? Which have not been?" Her hand moved from his cheek, and she wrapped her arms around his neck.

"I still believe Jane smiles too much, but now after seeing her help you unman Wickham in the park and feeling her wrath having been found in a compromising position in the carriage the night of our betrothal, I find her smiles make me nervous for I do not know what she hides behind them."

Elizabeth shook her head and laughed.

"And Mary is still far more severe than I should like to see in a young lady, but her thoughts run deep and true. A more steady moral light to follow may never be found. Her husband's parishioners will be blessed by her guidance." He closed his eyes. "Her husband is still odious."

She smiled up at him impertinently. "No redeeming qualities for Mr Collins?"

He shook his head. "I am afraid his only good quality is his wife."

Again she laughed.

"And then there is my impression of you." He

kissed her lightly on the forehead. "It has never wavered. Your eyes still enchant me, your laugh and smile are still bewitching, and your figure still tempts me beyond all rational thought." He bent his head and kissed her softly. "You remain now as you were then, the loveliest of all women." He again kissed her gently at first, then deepening it. His hands moved of their own volition caressing her back and pressing her closer to him. His lips trailed along her jaw and down her neck. "My sweetest, loveliest Elizabeth," he murmured as she sighed with pleasure. Reluctantly he drew back and rested his forehead on hers.

She tightened her grip on him, holding him as close as she possibly could. To be here with him, encircled within his arms was the most comforting of places. She could not imagine why her mother had ever told her a man's affections must be endured. To her, the attentions of her husband were something to be relished, and, she thought with a contented sigh, she had not yet experienced all of them. Her cheeks grew rosy at the thought, and she considered what she might talk about to keep her mind from wandering down that path. Before she could decide, he had scooped her into his arms and carried her to a chair where he sat with her in his lap.

She giggled as he arranged her in his arms.

"What do you find so humorous?" he asked.

"I was thinking of Jane, and that night in the carriage." She rested her head on his shoulder. "You only heard a small portion of the lecture I received. She is nearly as good as Mary at giving a moralizing sermon."

He chuckled. "As I said, I fear what she hides behind her pleasant facade."

Another giggle escaped her. "Do you suppose your friend has learned to be so wise?"

"No. He often sees only the good in people. Rarely does he recognize their faults until they are shown to him."

"And that is why he values your opinion so highly?"

Darcy shrugged. "Perhaps. Or perhaps it is why I value his companionship as much as I do. He helped me see the world from a brighter perspective when times were very dark indeed."

Elizabeth lifted her head and gave him a quizzical look. "When your sister fell victim to Wickham?"

He nodded. "And when my father passed. And when Richard was sent to war for the first time. Had I not had a light-hearted friend to cheer me, I might have turned into a very foul-tempered gentleman. Richard has likewise filled that role amiably. I could not ask for two better friends. They are more brothers than friends."

"They are very pleasant company, and I do enjoy how your countenance lightens when they are around. I imagine you might even tease each other and such when others are not around?"

"We do."

"I should like to experience that." Noting his look of confusion she clarified. "I would not be averse to your teasing me on occasion."

"You wish for me to tease you?"

She nodded. "On occasion. But, you must realize that teasing will lead to retaliation at times."

"Very well. I shall attempt to tease you on occasion and will strive not to be too cranky when the favour is returned."

She laughed. "I imagine you are a very patient gentleman. You have not only endured your cousin and friend for so many years; you have also survived Miss Bingley."

"Not without grumbling and an occasional drink, I can assure you."

"Well then, I shall make sure the cabinet never runs dry. I did not know I had married a man given to such vices." She gave him an impertinent smile.

"Mrs. Darcy..." he began but was stopped by her fingers being pressed against his lips.

"Say it again," she said. "But this time with less scolding in your tone." She lifted her fingers slightly.

"Mrs. Darcy..." he began only to be stopped once more by her fingers upon his lips.

She sighed. "I do like the sound of that. Especially when it is you saying it." She lifted her fingers and pressed her lips against his instead. "Now, what did you wish to say to me, husband." She sighed again. "I do like the sound of that, too. Husband."

"Hmmm..." he kissed her. "I have never been a man given to vice, my dear. I do not over indulge in spirits except on occasion. And those occasions usually involved my cousin." He kissed her again. "I do believe you may have come upon an even better remedy for my aversion to being teased." He was about to kiss her yet again when there was a scratching at the door, and Elizabeth quickly climbed off his lap. "They will not enter until I have allowed it." He stood and pulled her back into his embrace. "And I shall not allow it just yet."

When the third scratch came at the door some minutes later, Darcy took Elizabeth's hand and placed it in the crook of his arm. "Shall we go to dinner?"

~*~*~*~*~*~

Elizabeth rolled to her side and watched the rise and fall of her husband's chest. She sighed and snuggled into her pillow just a little more, pulling the blankets closer to her chin. She had enjoyed a peaceful moment of awakening and watching him sleep for nearly eight months now. She reached out a hand and traced his bottom lip with her finger. He smiled and captured her hand, kissing it before holding it against his heart.

"Good morning, my love," she whispered near his ear.

"Mmmm. Good morning." His eyes slowly opened, and he tugged her closer to his side. Letting go of her hand, he began to rub her arm, stopping to trace the scar. He kissed her forehead.

"Morning can never be anything but good with you to greet me."

She giggled as his hand slid around her waist tickling her in the process. "Have you forgotten we are not at home? There may be much to distress you this morning no matter how determined you are to be content."

"Aunt Catherine can be a challenge, but as long as she treats you well, I shall be satisfied." He released his hold on Elizabeth and sat up. "However, there is no need to deliberately vex her. She was insistent last evening on breaking her fast with us, so I suggest we appear in the breakfast room soon." He sighed loudly. Although he had, upon Elizabeth's insistence, made peace with his aunt, he found it hard to forget the way she had treated Elizabeth. "I do not know why she cannot breakfast at the dower house and call upon us later."

Elizabeth scooted behind him and wrapped her arms around his chest, propping her chin on his shoulder. "Are you sure you do not wish to vex her?" She ran her fingers softly across his chest.

He laughed and shook his head. "It may not be the choice I prefer, but I do believe it to be the wisest choice." He threw the covers back and removed himself from her embrace. "Have you forgotten that your mother and sisters are to call today? You may wish to have some sustenance before enduring your mother's raptures. Especially since you have news which will increase them."

She shrugged. "I had hoped to avoid them completely by hiding in my room with my husband until she returns to Longbourn. Then I could put my news in a letter. I am sure I would still hear the shrieking from here, but it would be considerably more bearable."

"Ah, where is my brave Lizzy?" he asked bending to give her a kiss. "I promise to be your second should you require it, which you will not." He crossed the room to the bell pull. "You may wish to sneak into your room before my man comes."

"Or you could hand me my robe."

"I could." He took the robe from the chair beside him. "Here it is." He held it out but made no move toward the bed.

"But I cannot reach it from here."

He grinned. "I know."

"And I am not..." she looked down at her state of undress.

His grin grew. "Yes, I know that, too."

She let out a huff and scurried from the bed to where he stood holding her robe open for her. He wrapped it around her and kissed her very soundly before pulling the bell. "I knew my brave Lizzy was in there."

She hurried toward her room but turned to give him a playful glare. "You do realize I shall make you pay?"

"Well, I had hoped you would."

Laughing, she opened the door to her room.

~*~*~*~*~*~

Elizabeth snuggled her nephew close rubbing his head and murmuring in his ear.

"You look quite content, Lizzy," said Mary taking a seat next to her. "John is a good baby. William and I have indeed been blessed." She gave her sister a knowing look. "Have you told Mama yet about your little one?"

Elizabeth shook her head. "I intend to tell her this visit, but I am not sure I am ready for her elations."

Mary chuckled. "Or her advice. She has as much advice as Lady Catherine and none of it is terribly useful." She patted her sister's knee. "Lord Bladen was unable to suffer the constant stream of advice and had Lady Catherine moved to the dower house within a month of the announcement. Anne has fared much better since. I had feared for her at first, she was so sickly. And as you can see, she is looking well."

Indeed, Anne was the picture of a glowing mother-to-be. She sat in the shade. Her feet elevated on a cushion and her hand resting lightly on her very round belly. "She has three months?"

"Yes, there shall be a new heir by Christmas." Richard followed by Darcy brought chairs close to join the ladies. "It seems none of us will win any bets. Our child will not be here until after twelfth night and Bingley's just before. Who would have thought Anne and Thad would be first?"

"Not I," said Elizabeth. "But you forgot to list one. It seems Pemberley will have an heir in March."

Richard looked between Elizabeth and Darcy before letting out a whoop.

Mary took her crying son from Elizabeth walked toward the edge of the garden, jostling him and attempting to calm the startled child.

"Richard Fitzwilliam, you had better learn to not shout so around a sleeping child before ours arrives," said Charlotte as she and Anne made their way to where Elizabeth sat. "You told him your news?"

"I did."

"You knew?" Richard questioned his wife.

"Yes, there are things women speak about that they do not share with their husbands." She smoothed his hair away from his eyes. "Trust me, my dear, you do not wish to know about them."

"Off-putting are they?"

"Quite."

Spotting his brother and Bingley just making their way back from the fish pond, he called out to them. "Darcy will have an heir in March."

Elizabeth cringed at the delighted shriek she heard from her mother.

"You no longer need to wonder how to tell your mother," said Darcy. "Are there any other announcements, Richard, the town crier of Rosings, can make?"

"I can think of none which will distract my mother from her mission." She wound her arm about her husband's. "Are you ready to be my second and rescue me?"

"I shall plead for you to be allowed a rest in a quarter hour."

"Will I be allowed to hide in our room with my husband?"

"For as long as you like." He rose and bowed. "Mrs. Bennet, you may have my seat next to your daughter."

Elizabeth grabbed his hand. He smiled reassuringly at her. "Quarter hour," he said.

She nodded and turned to begin listening to her mother's elations and advice.

~*~*~*~*~*~

"You would think he had never done this before." Bingley folded the paper he had been reading and placed it his lap.

"Perhaps if he had been a bit more polite to the physician, he would not need to be pacing down here disturbing our peace," said Richard.

"I merely asked a few questions," said Darcy.

"Few questions?" scoffed Richard. "Yes, and the Inquisition was merely an interview."

"It was not that bad." Darcy glared at his cousin.

"Dr. Thompson is one of the most patient men I know, Darcy," said Bingley. "It had to have been more than a few questions for him to have banished you from the room."

Darcy sank into a chair. "But the baby was not supposed to come until next month. Neither Katie nor Fredrick was born so early. What if this child is not strong enough? What if Lizzy..." His voice trailed off as he leaned his head back against his chair and stared at the ceiling.

"Lizzy will be well," reassured his cousin, "and the baby, too. The earliness of the child's arrival may be due to simple calculation errors. It is always a bit of a gamble predicting the exact time of a birth."

Darcy sighed. "Yes, Dr. Thompson said the same before he suggested I wait down here."

The door to the library opened.

"I do not need to be announced. He is my nephew; I should hope he knows who I am." Lady Catherine stood one hand on the door, the other shooing Darcy's butler away. "It would be much more beneficial should you make ready the parlour for tea rather than introducing people who are already known. And these parcels," she motioned to the footman who accompanied her. His arms were laden with half a dozen packages, all tied prettily with bows of varying colours. "They should be placed in that room as well." She tapped her walking stick on the floor and waited until she knew her instructions were being carried out. Then, she entered the room.

"How is my niece, Darcy?" She handed her walking stick to Bingley as she motioned for Richard to assist her with her wrap. "I was under the impression she wished for you to attend her at this event—ridiculous notion, but I could not disabuse her of it. You are not shirking your duties, are you?"

"I have been asked to wait here until I am summoned."

She tilted her head and narrowed her eyes as she studied him. "Causing grief for the physician or your wife?"

A chuckle escaped Richard. "Both, I assume."

Lady Catherine clucked her tongue and shook her head. "How you ever were fortunate enough to have her agree to marry the likes of you...always needing to know every detail and demanding that things be done your way. Preposterous! Who lives that way?"

"I can think of at least one aunt," said Darcy.

"Yes, well," said Lady Catherine. "A lady of my advanced years is expected to be set in her ways."

"It is not a recent affliction," muttered Darcy.

"More likely a family trait," said Lady Matlock, who had just recently entered the room. "Your Uncle is no better. He must know all and insists on things being done his way." She crossed the room and greeted first Richard with a kiss and then Darcy. "It is a trying time to be sure."

"Now," said Lady Catherine. "Although it is good to see you, Darcy, we are not here for you. Today is a momentous day for young Miss Darcy for today she is to become an older sister."

"Did you not celebrate that when Fredrick was born?" Darcy asked.

"Indeed. But do you wish for her to favour Fredrick over the new child? No, it is better we celebrate them all. Of course, if the celebrations are too much for you to endure every two years, you could stop procreating. Now, do make yourself useful and fetch your daughter. We are to have tea and presents."

Darcy rose to do as he was bid, but Lady Matlock stayed him. "There is no need, Darcy. I have already sent for her."

Just then, a small girl of four with brown hair and large blue eyes entered the room. "Papa!" She squealed as she made straight for him. "Papa, I am to have a party."

"Yes, I have heard," said Darcy scooping her up. "Aunt Catherine and Aunt Elaine were telling me that you were going to have tea..."

"And presents!" She clapped her hands.

"Yes, presents," Darcy said with a sigh and a pleading look to his Aunt Elaine.

"Oh, we have presents for more than just you, sweetheart, " said Lady Matlock taking the child from her father. "We have gifts for you to give as well."

"I get to give presents?" Her eyes were wide in surprise. "I like giving presents."

"Better than getting them?" asked Lady Matlock with a wink to Darcy. She understood his worry that his child would be spoiled by the frequent gifts Lady Catherine bestowed upon her.

Katie, Katherine Elizabeth Darcy, scrunched up her face and thought for a moment before shaking her head. "No, but it is almost as good." She played with the brooch on Lady Matlock's dress. "Can I give one to Mama?"

"Later after she and the new baby have had a good sleep. You can give them to your papa, and he will let you know when you can give them to your mama." They continued to discuss the gifts and whether there would be gingerbread to eat with the tea as they left the room.

"You know, I still cannot quite fathom the change in our Aunt Catherine," said Richard. "To think she was so set against your marrying Elizabeth and now it is you who must bear her disapprobation while your wife and daughter appear to be favourites."

Darcy laughed. "I do not mind bearing her disapproval if it means her acceptance of Elizabeth."

Lady Catherine's acceptance of Elizabeth had been gradual. Over the last five years, there had been more than one night, he had comforted his wife after a particularly trying experience involving his aunt. But, acceptance had come and continued to grow.

Lady Catherine's improvement was not all that had changed in those five years. Georgiana had taken her place in society and was now married. Richard and Charlotte had three boys and his venture into raising horses was a resounding success.

Bingley and Jane had two sweet girls and had settled into an estate not far from Pemberley in Derbyshire. Caroline resided with the Hursts and was
currently betrothed to a wealthy widower and
associate of Mr. Gardiner. Thaddeus and Anne
still resided at Rosings and were the parents of two
boys. Mr. Collins was still their clergyman. He and
Mary had just recently welcomed their fourth son
into their home. Mr. and Mrs. Bennet still resided
at Longbourn though Mr. Bennet's health often
took them to Bath; much to the delight of Lydia,
who found country living was not as delightful as
being surrounded by people. Kitty no longer lived
at Longbourn. Her home was now in Kent, having
found a match on one of her visits to the parsonage
at Hunsford.

The Gardiners still lived in Gracechurch
Street. Andrew had his eyes set on following in
the footsteps of his father. He approached the task
with great seriousness and truly was turning into
a very fine gentleman. Michael retained his love of
boats and seemed destined to be part of the merchant fleet.

Much had changed over the years, but one

thing had not. Darcy was as besotted with his wife now as he had always been.

"Mr. Darcy, your wife has requested your presence." A young maid stood just inside the library door, her voice interrupting his rumination.

"Ah, your banishment is over," teased Richard. "Do remember to come tell us whether we are uncles to a niece or a nephew."

"As soon as I am able," called Darcy over his shoulder.

~*~*~*~*~

Elizabeth dozed while her new daughter lay by her side. The baby squirmed and made suckling noises. Carefully, Darcy picked her up.

"Your mama is tired, little one." He cuddled her close. "God has given you the best mama, you know. She is beautiful and brave and very, very lovely."

Elizabeth smiled and placed a hand on his arm. It was the very same speech he had given each of their children at their birth and repeated to them often as he would kiss them good night.

"Shh. She is sleeping, and you should be, too. Katie has been promised a chance to give you and her sister, Claire, gifts but not until you have rested." He kissed his daughter's head.

Elizabeth held out her arms. "Give her to me, so that you may lie down and hold us both. I know it shall help me sleep much better, for I am always so much more at peace with you by my side."

"As am I." He handed the sleeping baby to her and removing his boots and jacket, lay down beside her wrapping both her and their daughter in his arm. "Elizabeth?" He whispered.

"Mmm hmm," she murmured sleepily.

"Thank you."

"For what?" she asked.

"For our children. For your love. But most of all, for vexing your mother enough to disturb your father's peace."

She giggled softly. "Then perhaps you should thank Mr. Collins."

He chuckled. "I do love you, Mrs. Darcy."

"And I love you, Mr. Darcy."

And who can be in doubt that what followed was a very happy life.

Acknowledgements

Thank you to the many people who have shared in the creation of this work.

To thank all the readers and friends who have encouraged me on this journey would be nearly impossible. However, I would be remiss if I did not mention a few. First, there is my invaluable team of beta's, Aino, Kathryn, and Rose, who checked facts, story elements, punctuation, spelling and grammar. Then, there is Sarah, who did such beautiful work on my cover. Next, I must thank Kathleen, who encouraged me to take on the task of transforming a very rough first draft into the story it is today. And I mustn't forget Zoe, who cheered me on when my courage was flagging. Finally, and most importantly, I must thank my husband for his loving and somewhat pushy support of my writing–without his insistence that I share my work, this book may not have come to be.

FOR PEACE OF MIND

Other Books by Leenie Brown

OXFORD COTTAGE

Elizabeth Bennet expects to complete the challenge her father has set before her at Oxford Cottage. What she does not expect is to meet a handsome stranger and fall in love, nor does she expect to find herself in a situation where she will have to keep both herself and her young companion safe.

TEATIME TALES

A collection of six short and sweet Jane Austen-inspired stories intended to be a light pick-me-up.

LISTEN TO YOUR HEART

When Anne de Bourgh finds some hidden papers,
her view of the future changes in light of her
father's wishes.

Her declaration to follow her heart and choose
her own future causes discord and forces secrets
to be revealed. Sometimes the path to happily
ever after can be strewn with danger and intrigue.

THROUGH EVERY STORM

Wickham is a changed man, but his wife has yet to
leave some of her childish ways behind. Can a
former wastrel redeem both himself and his wife?

HER FATHER'S CHOICE

Book 1 in the Choices Series
Sometimes a father knows what is best for his
child. At least Mr. Bennet trusts he does. Seeing
the potential of a good match for his beloved Lizzy
but knowing her ability to hold a grudge, he puts a
plan into action that forces a marriage between
Darcy and Elizabeth.

NO OTHER CHOICE

Book 2 in the Choices Series
Mary Bennet has never been the center of attention and rarely the object of any man's affections, but that is about to change. Shortly after Darcy and Elizabeth's wedding, Mary travels to London to prepare for the season, a season she is determined to finish with either a husband or a glorious tale to tell, even if it means learning to tolerate Lord Rycroft.

HIS INCONVENIENT CHOICE

Book 3 in the Choices Series
Colonel Fitzwilliam has always known his father would try to force him into a marriage of convenience, but after Kitty Bennet captures his heart as she shivered in the cold on the streets of Meryton, he realizes his only chance at happiness lies in making an inconvenient choice. However, it is a choice that will not go unchallenged. As family secrets are revealed, it is a choice that, in creating happiness for the colonel, could destroy his family.

HER HEART'S CHOICE

Book 4 in the Choices Series
To Anne, it had seemed simple enough. Place an advertisement in the paper, interview the gentlemen who responded, and select the best husband. But nothing is as easy as it seems. Indeed, many things are quite the opposite of how they appear. How is a lady to find a safe and secure marriage when her ideals are turned on their head — especially when her heart yearns for a man who is wholly unsuitable?

AND THEN LOVE

A Pride and Prejudice Prequel - Willow Hall Romance, Book 1
Events from the past combined with threats in the present threaten to tear Lucy and Philip apart unless Darcy can help his friends save their blossoming love and rid Lucy of her uncle once and for all.

FINALLY MRS. DARCY

After being separated for years, it takes very little time for Darcy and Elizabeth to come to an understanding and for Elizabeth to discover the true reason for their separation. Is a complete restoration of relationships possible, or will their happily ever after always be tainted by separation?

About the Author

Leenie Brown has always been a girl with an active imagination, which, while growing up, was a both an asset, providing many hours of fun as she played out stories, and a liability, when her older sister and aunt would tell her frightening tales. At one time, they had her convinced Dracula lived in the trunk at the end of the bed she slept in when visiting her grandparents!

Although it has been years since she cowered in her bed in her grandparents' basement, she still has an imagination which occasionally runs away with her, and she feeds it now as she did then — by reading!

Her heroes, when growing up, were authors, and the worlds they painted with words were (and still are) her favourite playgrounds! She was that child, under the covers with the flashlight, reading until the wee hours of the morning...and pretending not to be tired the next day so her mother wouldn't find out.

In addition to feeding her imagination, she also exercises it — by writing. While writing has been an activity she has dabbled in over the years, it blossomed into a full-fledged obsession when she stumbled upon the world of Jane Austen Fan Fiction. Leenie had first fallen in love with Jane Austen's work in her early teens when she was captivated by the tale of a girl, who like her, was the second born of five daughters. Now, as an adult, she spends much time in the regency world, playing with the characters from her favourite Jane Austen novels and a few that are of her own creation.

When she is not traipsing down a trail in an attempt to keep up with her imagination, Leenie resides in the beautiful province of Nova Scotia with her two sons and her very own Mr. Brown (a wonderful mix of all the best of Darcy, Bingley and Edmund with a healthy dose of the teasing Mr. Tilney and just a dash of the scolding Mr. Knightley).